Flower Power Fatality

A Psychedelic Spy Mystery
(Book 1)

by

Sally Carpenter

For information, email Cozy Cat Press, cozycatpress@aol.com or visit our website at: www.cozycatpress.com

COZY CAT
P R E S S

ISBN: 978-1-946063-54-0
Printed in the United States of America

Cover design by Paula Ellenberger
www.paulaellenberger.com

10 9 8 7 6 5 4 3 2 1

Dedicated to Peter Graves, 1926-2010,
television's greatest secret agent

Acknowledgements

A cozy set in 1967? And why not? The era was colorful time of high fashion, pop art, new music and offbeat movies. Societal attitudes, for better or worse, were changing. While the hippies were chanting "peace and love" and "drop out," the country was reeling with an unpopular war, civil rights marches, youth rebellion, the women's movement, assassinations, the space race, Communist spies and the threat of nuclear war. It was a volatile time full of energy and conflict—except in my boring (as I remember it) hometown.

For this book I started with my memories of growing up in the 1960s in a small, Midwest rural town. Many people of the time continued to embrace the values of the 1950s. Most citizens of the time did not wear tie-dye all the time or run off to live on hippie communes. Some readers may have had a different experience of life in the 1960s and that's okay.

I tried to stay true to the attitudes of the age, so some of the dialogue may not sound "politically correct" to modern ears. But to force contemporary speech onto characters of the past would be a disservice to history and to readers.

The fictitious town of Yuletide was inspired by the real-life burg of Santa Claus, Indiana, home of the world's oldest theme park formerly known as Santa Claus Land, now Holiday World and Splashin' Safari. The family owned-and-operated park is still a big tourist draw today.

The character of Rambler first appeared in the Cozy Cat Press group mystery *Chasing the Codex*. I liked him so much it seemed a shame not to use him in another story.

My thanks, as always, to my publisher, Patricia Rockwell, who continues to provide an outlet for my off-the-wall writing.

The *Mission: Impossible* episode referenced in chapter 19 is "The Legacy," original air date January 7, 1967.

Chapter 1: Baby The Rain Must Fall
Saturday, 1967

The Winter Witch sneered at the elves of Santa's workshop during the evening performance. On the metal benches in front of the outdoor stage, a handful of families sat huddled against the light rain. The early morning sunshine had tricked the tourists, so they'd arrived at the Country Christmas Family Fun Park without rain slickers or umbrellas. From the stage, Noelle McNabb, dressed as the Witch in a floor-length black dress, waved her broomstick and yelled at her fellow cast members. From the corner of her eye, she spied the miserable guests scattered throughout the seats. Nothing was worse than playing to a near-empty house on an overcast day in April when most of the fine folk of Yuletide, Indiana, were snug in their cozy homes. Despite the temptation to rush through her lines so she could leave the stage, Noelle stayed in character.

"There'll be no Christmas this year!" She gave her most gruesome cackle, first to the elves and then the audience. Usually, the kids watching reacted to her, but this group was more interested in staying dry than in following the story. Blank stares greeted her scowl. The elves, played by high schoolers clad in colorful tights and leotards, cringed at the Witch's threat. Or were they just shivering from the cold wind?

"You mean . . . no presents?" asked one elf.

"No carols?" said another.

"No sleigh rides?" added a third.

Noelle let out her loudest evil laugh. She cranked up

her energy in an attempt to wake up the audience. "Indubitably! If I can't be glad, then I'll just stay mad, and everyone will be sad, with no Christmas cheer for anyone, from the oldest adult to the youngest lad!" If she could make this cornball dialogue sound good, she could handle any role.

The Witch chased the elves around the wooden stage that creaked beneath their footsteps. At least the movement kept her muscles from cramping. At six feet tall, Noelle towered over the young actors. She plucked the jingle bell cap off one elf and tossed it at the benches. The kids in the audience typically clamored to claim the cap for their own, but nobody moved. The overhead stage lights provided no heat against the chill. A roof above the stage kept the rain off Noelle, but the wind cut through her long-sleeved costume and blew raindrops onto her face. She touched her cheek. Was her green makeup running? Some day she'd have to ask the park director why the *Candy Cane Capers* show couldn't be moved indoors during inclement weather, which, in rural southwest Indiana, was most of the year.

"Special delivery!" An actor in a brown reindeer costume ran onto the stage. The papier-mâché deer head muffled his voice. "I have a special delivery for the Winter Witch!" He skidded to a stop beside Noelle. "Are you Miss Witch? Or just a miss fit?"

"My name fits me snug as a bug," she replied.

"I'm Rudolph, and I have a package for you from Santa!" He held out a large box wrapped in foil and ribbon.

"Phooey! For me? From Santa? He never gives me presents 'cause I'm a bad, bad girl." Noelle took the box and pressed her ear against it. "Hmmm, I hear ticking. Is it a bomb?"

One of the elves giggled. "If it's a gift for the witch, it's bound to be a dud!"

Another elf said, "Hey, witch, open the box and we'll have an explosive finish!"

No chuckles from the audience. Normally at this point, Noelle waited for the laughter to subside, but this soggy crowd wouldn't giggle if Rudolph dropped his furry pants. She jumped into her next line.

"Stand back, kiddies! If this is a bomb, we'll all be in orbit with Sputnik!" The reference to the space race usually sailed over the heads of the watching tykes, and, apparently for this show, their parents as well.

The elves rushed to the back of the stage and covered their faces with their hands. Noelle yanked off the box lid and reached it. She removed an ornate clock covered in holly. A card was tied to the clock.

"Tell us what it says," the reindeer asked.

"Don't rush me!" she replied. "I only have a third-grade education! If I had finished school, I wouldn't be so mean!" Noelle held up the card and pretended to read it. "It says, 'It's time for you to be a nicer person.'" She handed the clock to Rudolph and peered into the box. "But wait, there's more!" From the box she removed a baby doll. "Awww! If I'd had such a beautiful dolly when I was a little girl, I wouldn't have grown up into a cranky old witch! And look!" She raised the doll so the audience could see the huge red valentine heart sewn to its stuffed chest. "It's all heart!"

Rudolph said, "Yeah, you can have heart-to-heart talks with your new dolly friend!" Then he spoke directly to the audience. "And you can have one too. Heart-full dolls are available at Santa's Bag gift shop right here in the park!"

The crass commercialism annoyed Noelle more than the dopey script, but she carried on like a professional. "Gosh, yes! And I've been so heartless to my friends, the elves." She moved to the front of the stage and spoke directly to the audience, "And it's time for all of us to be nicer to our friends and families, isn't it?"

Rudolph stood beside her. In the humid weather his shaggy costume emitted a strong musty odor. "It sure is! And remember, kids, nobody is so bad that a little love won't fix him!"

The Witch and Rudolph stepped aside so the elves could come downstage for the closing musical number. Children dressed as snowflakes entered from the wings and joined the dance. A couple of the dancers slipped on the wet stage. When finished, everyone froze in place for the usual audience applause, which tonight consisted of guests slapping their hands together in an effort to stay warm. After a quick group bow the cast rushed off stage into the wings and down the stairs to the basement dressing rooms.

Seated at her mirror in the women's dressing room, Noelle tossed the witch's hat onto the makeup counter. She pulled off her wig and brushed her brown hair. She'd recently had her long tresses cut into a smart bob with a small pointed curl plastered on each cheek. Keeping up with the latest hairstyles in this hick town was a challenge. The other female cast members still wore their hair long and straight.

The overhead fluorescent light flickered. "Brrrr! It's colder in here than outside!" said one of the girls.

Another elf stripped off her damp costume. "Yeah, you know old man Ferguson," the owner/director of the theme park. "He can buy billboards for the highways, but he can't afford heat for his slaves."

While Noelle rubbed her face with cold cream to remove the green makeup, the girls changed into their street clothes and chattered. At age 25, Noelle was the oldest cast member and as such seldom socialized with the "kids," as she called them. Many of the park employees came from the local schools. When school was in session, the park was only open weekends, due to fewer tourists and the schedules of the younger workers. After graduation most of the older youths moved on to other jobs, college, marriage or the armed forces, but a constant crop of new kids kept the park positions filled.

"Thank goodness that was the last show of the day," one girl said. "I'm going home to warm up in a hot tub."

"Why does Fergy keep the park open in spring when it rains every day?" said another.

"We're lucky he does." Noelle pulled off her fake bushy eyebrows. "We don't get paid when the park's closed."

The girls didn't care about money because they lived with their parents and spent their wages on clothes and movies. But Noelle needed her earnings for rent and food.

"It won't matter to you, Noelle, when you become a big movie star. You'll have a swimming pool full of cash!" The girl laughed.

Another one took up the jest. "Yeah, Noelle, in Los Angeles it's hot and sunny all the time and you won't have to do shows in the rain!"

Noelle turned to face them, her blue eyes blazing. "At least I have dreams! If the rest of you want to rot away in this wide-spot-in-the-road for the rest of your lives, be my guest!"

The other girls had finished dressing. They left their dirty costumes on the floor, which they knew was against the rules. One said, "Let's go so the drama queen can polish her Oscar." The girls giggled on their way out the door.

Alone at last. Noelle was glad to be rid of the immature urchins but sadden by her status. She planned to move to Hollywood as soon as she'd saved enough money, but on her meager park wages that could take years. The ceiling lights hummed, and the steam radiator banged. The empty room had an eerie feel. Having the most makeup to remove, Noelle was always the last one out the door at the end of a long workday. With her face clean, she rested her elbows on the Formica counter and starred into the light-rimmed mirror.

"Mirror, mirror on my table, who's the fairest hard luck actress of them all?" Was her skin starting to take on a green hue from the cosmetics? If she didn't get to the West Coast soon, the only role she'd be playing would be as a green bean in a vegetable commercial.

Noelle switched off the mirror lights and removed her street clothes from her metal wall locker. She changed into a warm pullover sweater and slipped a skirt over her pantyhose. She dropped the witch's costume into the hamper for the overnight laundry service to clean. Nimble fingers unwrapped her clear plastic rain bonnet and tied the straps under her chin. At least she had brought her raingear, thanks to watching her cousin, the WOWS-TV weather girl, the night before. With her knee-high vinyl boots she didn't need those ugly plastic rain boots her mom pestered her to wear. Noelle slipped on her raincoat, picked up her purse, turned off the ceiling lights and shut the dressing room door behind her.

Darkness had fallen, and the theme park was closing for the night. On her way to the staff parking lot, Noelle passed the carousel dislodging the last riders from the hand-painted wooden ponies. Didn't Fergy worry about the electrical systems short-circuiting in the rain? The lights on the merry-go-round switched off, and the taped hurdy-gurdy organ music abruptly ceased. The shopkeepers of the various buildings rolled down the metal shutters over the service windows. In the center of the park, the sparkly lights on the twenty-foot-tall living Christmas tree, kept decorated year-round, snapped off. The animal handlers herded the live reindeer from the open coral and into their stalls for the night.

As soon as Noelle was seated in her 1965 blue Volkswagen Beetle, the clouds let loose with the rain. At least the deluge had waited until the tourists had cleared the park. She turned on the headlights and windshield wipers before heading home in the gloom. On Kringle Avenue, the main drag through downtown, the sidewalks were empty, as the shops had closed for the day. On a Saturday night in Yuletide, the only signs of life could be found at the Lollipop Lanes bowling alley, the roller-skating rink, the single-screen Holiday Cinema or The Barn dance hall.

"Strawberry Fields Forever," The Beatles' most recent single, played on the car radio. Noelle kept her radio dial set on the rock-and-roll station that broadcasted from Riverbend, the metropolis five miles south, but her parents preferred WEEK-AM, the hometown station with its format of easy listening and farm reports.

The music faded out for the news. "The top story this hour: This afternoon about a hundred students from Ohio River College in Riverbend gathered in Veterans Park to protest the Vietnam War. The demonstration began peaceably as the students sang anti-war songs and carried placards. But the protest turned chaotic as about dozen young men set a fire in a trash bin and burned their draft cards. The demonstrators then lit firecrackers to throw at the local law enforcement. The police broke up the riot and arrested several protesters."

Nothing exciting like that ever happened in this humdrum town. Noelle turned onto to a two-lane country road, expertly dodging the potholes. She stopped beside two metal mailboxes sharing a wooden post. One mailbox belonged to her landlords. Her box was labeled 113A Ornament Lane. Her landlords, the occupants of the larger house on the property, were out of town on one of their frequent trips, so she picked up their mail to give to them later. Noelle didn't check the plastic newspaper holder beneath the mailboxes as the *Yuletide Herald* was only published on weekdays. She pulled onto the gravel driveway that wound past the main house and went deep into the wooded acreage. At the end of the drive stood the one-bedroom cottage and a one-car detached garage that she rented. A modest pad, but at least she had her own space away from her parents and annoying siblings.

At the sound of her car engine, a fat black cat ran from the woods. Noelle slammed on the brakes to avoid hitting the animal as it stopped smack in front of the car. Exasperated, she rolled down the window and poked out her head.

"Ceebee! Will you move! I have to park!"

The cat stared, the headlights reflecting in its yellow eyes.

"Don't make me come out there and get you!"

They'd played this game many times before. Noelle threw the stick shift into park, stepped out of the car and pushed up the garage door. Then she picked up the cat and deposited him on the passenger seat. Ceebee clawed the car seat. Noelle parked the Bug inside the garage as the rain blew in. With purse and cat in hand, she pulled down the garage door and hurried along the concrete walkway to the front door, ducking her head to keep the rain out of her face. She had the foresight earlier in the day to leave on the porch light so she could see the way after dark. Ceebee jumped from her arms and pressed against the screen door so she couldn't open it. Noelle yanked the door open hard enough to push Ceebee aside, then held the screen door open with her hip so she could unlock the front door. Ceebee rubbed on her legs and fussed.

"All right, I can't feed you until I get inside, okay?"

Once the door was open, the feline raced inside and left watery paw prints across the linoleum floor. The actress shut the door and snapped on the ceiling light as Ceebee yowled.

"Will you hush! Can I at least get my raincoat off?"

More meowing from Ceebee, as he pawed at her legs.

"Don't get your muddy paws on my boots!" She dropped her purse on the coffee table in the living room. "All right, I'll feed your bottomless pit. Honestly, if you're so hungry, go catch a mouse."

Noelle headed for the kitchenette with the cat on her heels. She opened a wall cabinet and removed a frosted white Tupperware container full of dry cat chow. She filled a ceramic cat bowl with chow as Ceebee bounced around her ankles. After she set the bowl on the floor, Ceebee dug in. Noelle leaned over to pet him.

"Yeww! You're soaking wet! Couldn't you go inside your cathouse and stay dry? Silly poo!"

Her dad had built a little wooden house outside where Ceebee could escape the cold Hoosier winters, but during rainstorms the cat preferred to sit under a tree. Noelle pulled some paper towels off the wooden towel rack and wiped Ceebee. The cat purred as he inhaled the food.

"How's my little cat burglar, huh? Did you have fun running around outside?" She had named him Ceebee because of his tendency to snatch anything that wasn't nailed down.

Noelle shivered, not just from her wet clothes but also from the damp cold inside the house. But satisfying the cat always came first, even before switching on the heat. After tossing the wet paper towels into the waste can, Noelle turned up the round thermostat dial on the wall and the furnace kicked on. In the bathroom she dropped her soggy rain bonnet into the sink and hung the raincoat on the shower curtain rod to drip dry over the tub. But before she could change into dry clothes, from the kitchenette came a pitiful "mew."

"The vet said you shouldn't eat so much. You're too fat."

After another "mew," a handful of kibble found its way into the bowl. Now that the cat had a full tummy, Noelle could finally take care of her own needs. She retreated into the bedroom and changed into flannel pajamas, a terrycloth robe and slippers.

The rain pattered on the windows as Ceebee vigorously washed his face. On a wall in the kitchenette, a black Felix The Cat clock ticked away with the cat's tail and eyes moving back and forth with each tock. Noelle set the empty cat food bowl in the porcelain sink and lit two burners on the gas stove. She put on a pan on one burner to cook a grilled cheese sandwich made with white bread and Velveeta cheese slices. On the other burner she heated a can of Campbell's cream of tomato soup with a cup of whole milk stirred in. A bowl of cherry Jell-O with fruit cocktail mixed in topped off the meal.

Noelle carried the food into the living room and set it on the metal TV tray in front of the sofa. She closed the window curtains and switched on the TV set that sat on a wheeled stand. She adjusted the long, wire "rabbit ear" antenna to tune in the fuzzy picture. Often the electricity went out during rainstorms, causing Noelle to miss the conclusions her favorite shows and then waiting until summer reruns to find out what happened. Noelle settled on one end of the couch—Ceebee hogged the middle, as usual—and ate dinner while the WOWS-TV local evening news unfolded in shades of gray on the black-and-white TV. The top story of the draft card burning in Riverbend included film footage of the participants.

After several ho-hum stories, weather girl Mamie Sprinkle finally came on. Thanks to the gal's nutty but accurate forecasts, the station enjoyed the highest news ratings in the city. Dressed in casual pants and tops, Mamie, along with her folksy manner and black ponytail, provided a welcome change from the drab, suit-and-tie weathermen on the other local stations.

The weather segment opened with the forecaster standing, as usual, before her white plastic-coated wall map of the USA. She held an armful of stuffed toy animals. "Well, folks, it's raining cats and dogs out there, but of course you already know that unless you're living in a cave. If you have to go out tonight, put on a slicker and put out some tuna for all the kitties pouring down."

Mamie set aside the toys, picked up some black and red felt-tipped markers, and attacked the map for some serious weather prognostication. She drew in swirls of airstreams, dabs of raindrops, jags of lightening and arcs of fast-moving storm fronts. For travelers, Mamie wrote in the high temps across the nation. Soon her sketches filled the map. After the broadcast ended, she'd wiped the board clean to start fresh the next day. The weather girl predicted the rain would ease up soon, with on-and-off light showers throughout the following week.

When Mamie finished, Noelle turned off the set. The sports news followed, which didn't interest her. After washing the dinner dishes, she heated up some milk and whisked in cocoa powder, vanilla extract and a pinch of salt for some delicious hot chocolate to warm her up. With mug in hand, she sat in the recliner chair in the living room to read the day's mail that included a letter from a fellow Class of 1964 alumnus from the Indiana State University theater department. The envelope contained a brief note and a newspaper clipping. Her friend was appearing in a new play at a small theater in Chicago, and the clipping contained a glowing review of her performance. Noelle was happy for her classmate, but she still felt a twinge of envy. She longed for rave reviews too. Someday she'd give a performance that would set the critics clapping and put her on the road to stardom.

Noelle finished off the hot cocoa and tossed the mail onto the growing stack of newspapers, magazines and envelopes atop the coffee table. She scooped Ceebee off the sofa.

"Time for your lesson."

She fetched a bag of cat treats from the kitchenette and squatted on the floor. Ceebee sat facing her. Holding a treat in her left hand, Noelle held out her right hand. "Shake." The cat raised his right paw level with her hand. Noelle shook the paw and held out the treat, which he gulped down. Noelle repeated the command; Ceebee obeyed each time.

"Good boy! I'll take you to Hollywood with me and we can be in movies together. I'll be a big animal trainer along with Frank Inn. You can do tricks for the camera and we'll be famous. What do you say to that?"

Ceebee raised a back leg and licked his butt.

The Felix The Cat clock gave the time as 7:45 p.m., fifteen minutes until her favorite TV show began. Noelle put away the cat treats, lit the stove and dug out a pan of Jiffy Pop popcorn. Holding the container's wire handle, Noelle shook the pan over the hot burner until the foil cover expanded with popped kernels. When finished, she turned off the stovetop and retrieved an ice-cold Frostie root beer from the fridge. She uncapped the glass bottle, and filled a paper plate with her mom's homemade chocolate chip cookies. Her cookie stash was running low. She'd better get more next time she visited her folks. Noelle took the food into the living room and turned on the TV again, excited about the upcoming show. What nifty caper did the good guys have planned this week? She peeled back the foil on the Jiffy Pop and munched on the popcorn.

After the top-of-the-hour station identification, a hand lit a fuse with a match, and Lalo Schifrin's jazzy theme music played over a montage of scenes from tonight's episode of *Mission: Impossible*. Noelle's favorite character on the fast-paced spy show was Cinnamon Carter, played by Barbara Bain with style, poise and elegance. Noelle longed to star in her own TV show, maybe a thriller like *M:I*, and be a great actress like Barbara. If only dreams came true.

Just as the agents got the mission underway, someone pounded on the front door. Who could it be? Her friends and parents always called before dropping by.

"Who is it?" she said. The knocking grew louder. Couldn't the visitor at least wait until the commercial break? "Mom, Dad, is that you?"

No answer. Noelle headed for the door. If only she could pause the TV to avoid missing her show or somehow save the episode so she could watch it later. Ceebee hid under the sofa. Noelle pushed back the window curtain and peeked out. Under the glow of the porch light stood a man she didn't recognize. Average height, early 20s, dark hair below his ears, boyish face and good looking. Maybe his car had broken down or run out of gas. She'd call the Texaco station and get someone to come out and help. She knew better than to let strangers into her house.

Noelle cracked open the door. "Do you need a mechanic?"

A flash of lightening lit up the sky. The man said nothing, only moaned. His eyes were glazed with pain. One hand clutched his chest. The front of his black leather jacket glistened with rainwater—and blood.

He spoke in a whisper. "Help . . . me."

"Do you need a doctor?"

Noelle opened the door wider. The man fell forward, landing face down on the floor.

Chapter 2: This Boy

Noelle stared at the stranger until a cold gust of wind slapped her in the face and snapped her out of her trance. She rolled the man onto his back, grabbed beneath his armpits, and dragged him into the house, leaving a trail of water and dead leaves across the floor. She closed the door, and Ceebee peeked out from beneath the sofa. Noelle knelt beside the man and unzipped his jacket. Blood seeped from a small hole in his chest and pooled across his plaid shirt. Noelle remembered the first aid course she'd taken for a Girl Scout merit badge years ago. She rushed to the kitchen to grab a white dishtowel decorated with an appliqué of vegetables. She folded the towel and pressed it against the wound to staunch the bleeding.

"Can you hear me?" she said. "Who are you? What's your name? What happened to you?"

He stared up at her, eyes wide in shock.

"Don't be scared. I won't hurt you."

He moaned and closed his eyes. She leaned over to listen to his breathing. Shallow breaths, but better than none at all. The towel was soaked with blood, so she dropped it in the kitchen sink to wash later. Noelle fetched her first aid kit and opened the metal box. Using gauze and white medical tape, she made a bandage to cover the chest hole. None too pretty, but it would suffice. She put one of the sofa pillows beneath his head. From the bedroom closet she found a blanket to keep him warm. She dried his hair and face with a bath towel.

Noelle picked up the handset of the turquoise Princess phone on the coffee table. One of her neighbors was gabbing on the party line.

"Excuse me," she said. "Can I please cut in?"

"Hi, Noelle," said the widow neighbor. "We'll be off shortly."

These "shortlys" generally ran an hour or two. "I can't wait. It's an emergency."

The widow got testy. "Just wait your turn. On Tuesday you were talking a long time with your friend."

"That was only twenty minutes, and what are you doing keeping track of my calls? I'll only take a minute to call for the ambulance. Then you can have the line back."

"Muriel and I haven't chatted in coon's ages—"

"Look, I have someone here who's very sick, and if you don't get off the line right now, he's going to die on my living room floor!"

"Well, there's no need to get huffy about it." With that the widow hung up.

Noelle sighed and dialed "zero." "Hello, Sybil?" Everyone knew Sybil, the operator for the Yuletide phone network. "Noelle McNabb. Please send an ambulance to my place. And the police."

As Noelle was busy on the phone, Ceebee crept out from under the sofa. He sniffed the man. The cat pawed at the stranger's pants pocket and pulled out a wallet and another object. Ceebee grabbed the item in his teeth and carried it to his stash of treasures beneath the couch. Whenever Noelle mopped the floor, she discovered twigs, dead insects, bits of scrap paper and pieces of bird's nests in the cat's hiding spot.

With assurances that the ambulance was on the way, Noelle hung up the phone and switched off the TV. She'd missed too much of the program to catch up on the story and, besides, she had too much real-life drama on her hands.

She sat on the floor and held the man's hand. "You must be freezing. That's a nasty storm out there. Are you from around here?"

Even if he couldn't hear her, Noelle chatted away, mostly to calm her own nerves. So many questions she wanted to ask, but he was sleeping—or unconscious. She gently shook his shoulder, but his eyes never opened.

"Hang in there, buddy. Hang in there. The ambulance is on the way. You'll make it."

On an impulse, she got up, pushed back a curtain and peered out the window. The rural area had no streetlights, but the bright moon and abundant starlight lit up the countryside well enough to see the empty driveway. No car, motorcycle or bicycle. The Greyhound bus didn't run on Saturday nights. How did he arrive? A man with a hole in his chest couldn't walk far. Someone must have given the stranger a ride, then left him wounded on the side of the road. But why?

She shut the door and stepped on the wallet, thinking it must have fallen out of the man's pocket when she brought him inside. Noelle picked up the smudged, brown leather billfold. Normally she'd never snoop inside someone's personal belongings, but she had to learn more about this guy. The Indiana driver's license was issued to Kent Calvert at a Riverbend address. The wallet also held a card for the Riverbend Municipal Library, an expired student ID card, punch cards for free burgers at a couple of drive-ins, and a photo of a young, attractive blonde, most likely a girlfriend. No bus ticket or indication of his destination. Noelle also found a thick wad of money and counted out several hundred dollars in bills. Startled, she stuffed the money back into the billfold and tossed the wallet on the coffee table. Why was Kent carrying around so much money? Anyone who hit the road with that much cash would sensibly hide it in a money belt or use traveler's checks. But apparently whoever shot him wasn't after the money.

The wail of the ambulance pierced the silent night. Noelle opened the door. White headlights and a red flashing roof light cut through the rain. The ambulance, a white station wagon with a red cross painted on the side, stopped in front of the garage. Right behind the ambulance came Yuletide's lone police car, chugging along without red lights or siren. The city police were never in a hurry to get anywhere, as the local crime consisted mostly of kids shoplifting at the five-and-dime, weekend fights at The Barn or drunks wandering home from the Tipsy Tavern.

Two medics wearing gray rain ponchos opened the back hatch on the ambulance and pulled out a metal-and-canvas gurney. Once the medics were inside the house, they yanked the blanket off the man, loaded him onto the low gurney, and strapped him in. Chief Judd Whitlock entered the cottage, his bulk filling the doorframe. He remained there, his heavy-lidded eyes watching the medics at work.

"Chief, could you please close the door?" Noelle was annoyed. "You're letting in the cold air."

"I don't feel it." Of course, he didn't, not with a thick jacket buttoned over his black uniform and mounds of body fat. In his lean and mean days as the star quarterback on the Yuletide High School football team, Whitlock had scored the last-minute touchdown that garnered the Elves their one and only regional tournament win. But when a mediocre career as a college athlete produced no professional league offers, inactivity set in. With the leisurely patrolling of the town's quiet streets, his muscle had turned to flab.

"Don't you want to examine the body?" she asked.

"Is he dead?" The chief sounded perturbed at being called out on a stormy night.

"I don't think so. I hope not. But please close the door."

He took a step in and slammed the door. Three men—four counting the guy on the gurney, but he wasn't looking—were in Noelle's house, and she was clad only in her nightclothes. No wonder she was cold—and embarrassed. She pulled the robe closed and tied the sash belt. At least she wasn't clad in the skimpy Baby Doll shorts and top she wore on hot summer nights.

The cop crossed his arms over his beer gut. "What seems to be the problem?"

"He has a hole in his chest."

"Huh." Whitlock grunted as he squatted, one hand resting on a knee to steady his bulk. With the other hand he peeled back the bandage. "Looks like a bullet hole." With more wheezing, he stood. "He's not one of our local boys."

Noelle shot the cop a glance. He made Barney Fife look like a genius.

"Who is he?" he asked.

"His name is Kent Calvert," she replied.

"You know him?"

"No, I don't. I've never seen him before."

"But you know his name."

"I looked at his driver's license."

"If you don't know him, what's he doing here? Is he a boyfriend who had a tad too much to drink?"

She frowned. "Drunks don't have blood all over their shirts."

"Who shot him?"

"I was hoping you'd find out."

"Did you two have a lover's tiff?"

"Chief, I don't own a gun. Never have, never will. And like I said, he is not my boyfriend."

One of the medics asked them to move out of the way so they could load the man into the ambulance. Noelle sidestepped, but Whitlock remained still. He tried to pull in his gut as the medics squeezed past him. They couldn't open the door, so Whitlock stepped back without looking and bumped into a floor lamp. Noelle reached around him and grabbed the lamp just in time to keep it from crashing to the floor. The medics finally maneuvered the stretcher through the door.

Whitlock stuck his thumbs into his gun belt in an attempt to look authoritative, but he only appeared fatter. "All right, missy, that's all for now, but I'll be back with more questions."

"Fine. Maybe by then I'll have some answers." She laid the sarcasm on thick.

"You're copping quite an attitude. Your generation has no respect for the law."

"What do you expect, when you harass me every time I'm working at the record shop."

"I gotta keep my eye on you. You hang out too much with those no-good hippie freaks."

Noelle bit her tongue to keep from screaming. As much as she wanted to lash out and defend her friends, Whitlock had a gun and handcuffs.

"I don't smoke pot, if that's what you mean."

"Uh huh." He didn't sound convinced. "You live all alone, 'way out here away from town. Nobody can see what you're up to."

"If you want to search my house for drugs, go ahead. You can bust me for having a bottle of aspirin."

The chief sniffled and wiped his damp nose with the back of his hand. "Not tonight. I gotta get going."

Back to his warm bed, she figured. "Will you let me know what happens to Mr. Calvert?"

"Oh, sure, missy, sure." Whitlock didn't sound like he meant it.

The police chief finally trudged out of the house. The storm had eased into a drizzle, and the wind had calmed down. From the open doorway Noelle wrapped her arms around her chest, braving the night air, and watched the officer leave. Since his car was blocking the ambulance, the medics had driven onto the grassy yard to get back on the road. The heavy vehicle had left ruts in the wet ground. Just great. In the morning she'd have to dig out the snow shovel and smooth out the ground. Off in the distance, a pair of headlights shone and then, quick as a wink, vanished. Noelle blinked. Maybe her eyes were playing tricks on her in the dark. Who would park on the side of the road in this weather?

Alone at last, Noelle locked the door and sank onto the couch. With the visitors gone, Ceebee crawled out of hiding. Noelle took a swig of her now-flat root beer. Strange that Whitlock hadn't noticed Kent's wallet on the table, but just as well. If he had taken the billfold, he might have kept the money for himself. The medics would probably take the patient to the nearby St. Nicholas Hospital, so she'd deliver the wallet to the man in the morning. No need to hurry. In his condition, Kent Calvert would not be checking out any time soon.

Ceebee jumped in her lap. Noelle absently petted him as she gazed at the mess of mud and blood she needed to clean off the floor. Something bothered her. As an actress, she paid attention to faces, and now that she had time to think, she had seen Kent Calvert before.

But where?

Chapter 3: What Goes On
Sunday

Noelle McNabb couldn't breathe.

At first, she dreamed that she was gasping for air. As her brain scrambled to wake up, her difficulty became real. Still flat on her back, she opened her eyes. A big black blob, with yellow eyes inches from her own, stared back. The cat lay content on her chest, purring.

"Ceebee! You're suffocating me!"

She tried to sit up in the four-poster bed, but the cat had other ideas and held his ground. Rather than push off the pet, Noelle gave in and scratched behind his ears, which generated a louder rumble. Something was wrong. On Sundays she rarely woke up before the alarm went off. With one hand still petting, the other reached for the nightstand and felt around for the wind-up alarm clock. Mickey Mouse's clock hands pointed to the nine and the six.

"Shoot! I forgot to set the alarm. Ceebee, you gotta move. I have to get up. Move, please."

She'd already missed Sunday School, which had started fifteen minutes ago, and she'd likely be late for the ten-thirty church service as well. After the excitement last night, she'd had trouble getting to sleep despite drinking a glass of warm milk and taking a hot bath. And now she'd overslept. Noelle was dying to call the hospital to check on Kent Calvert's condition. She also wanted to throw on a coat and sneakers and, as she did most Sunday mornings, walk to the mailbox and pick up the Sunday edition of the Riverbend newspaper, which might have some information about her mysterious stranger. But her paper perusal would have to wait until later.

She pushed the feline off; Ceebee jumped back in place. A second attempt at dislodging the cat likewise failed. This required strategy. Noelle grabbed the left side of the quilt that covered her and waved it. Ceebee, thinking it was playtime, pounced on the wiggly quilt. Noelle used the brief interlude to sit up and stick her feet into the fuzzy slippers on the floor. The cat's purr turned into a "feed me!" yowl.

Noelle smoothed her hair and threw on her robe. Ceebee grabbed the robe's belt as it dangled. For such a fat cat, he moved quickly. Noelle yawned, tied the belt around her waist, and plodded to the kitchenette. The cat left the bed and wove around her legs, fussing.

"Yes, your highness, I'm getting your food. You'll have to wait until I get to the kitchen."

Noelle switched on the boxy radio that sat on a shelf above the sink in hopes of hearing some news about Kent. But on Sunday mornings, the radio stations only played gospel music and sermons. She filled Ceebee's bowl with cat chow, and the stainless-steel percolator with water. She measured two teaspoons of Maxwell House coffee into the pot's metal filter and plugged in the cord. No time for a hearty, nutritious breakfast like her mom made; she'd have to settle for coffee and a glass of Carnation Instant Breakfast. After giving Ceebee second helpings, she stirred cold milk into a glass of the chocolate mix. She opened the back door to let Ceebee out and turned off the radio. After gulping down "breakfast," she made do with a quick face washing and tooth brushing.

In the bedroom, Noelle put on a long-sleeved miniskirt with bold squares of purple and yellow. She'd bought the dress at the Raintree Mall in Riverbend. The big city's boutique stores carried more interesting fashions than the local mom-and-pop shops. She sat at the cosmetic table in the bedroom and slapped on her makeup: black eyeliner around the eyes, brown eyebrow pencil, blue eye shadow, rouge and pink lipstick. A touch of hairspray held her cheek curls in place. Next she put on yellow tights and white knee boots. For jewelry, she put on the gold locket her mom had given her for her eighth birthday, rings and gold earrings. A matching yellow pillbox hat and white gloves completed the ensemble. She quickly transferred the contents of her casual handbag to a black patent leather clutch and slipped on a black trench coat. On her way out the front door she stuffed Kent's wallet into the purse.

The storm of the night before had given way to sunshine peeking through the clouds and the clean smell of rain-washed air. Once in town, her Beetle turned onto Madonna Street and slid into the last remaining parking spot in the lot beside Bethlehem Community Church with its tall steeple. Old Beth, as it was affectionately called because it was the first church founded in the town, sat just across the street from Holy Nativity Catholic Church. These two congregations were the largest houses of worship in Yuletide. The black families attended Emmanuel AME, and the Baptists and Pentecostals had a tiny congregation apiece. The nearest synagogue was in Riverbend.

Noelle unbuttoned her coat as she rushed into the narthex of the colonial-style structure and bumped into the robed choir members lined up for the processional. She apologized, grabbed a bulletin from a surprised usher, and rushed into the sanctuary. The morning sunbeams lit the stained-glass windows that lined the room. The organist was just winding down the prelude music. Noelle had arrived in the nick of time. She slid into the pew where her parents and two younger siblings sat.

"Sorry I'm late," she whispered to her mother.

Mom's reply was, "Your dress is too short."

Noelle tugged at the hem and sighed. Her parents just didn't appreciate nice clothes. Dad was in his standard dark suit and tie and white shirt; Mom wore one of her below-the-knee frowzy dresses from years ago. The organist fired up some loud chords, the signal for the congregation to stand for the opening hymn. Noelle jumped to her feet, snatched a hymnal from the pew rack, and flipped the pages. She sang the familiar song from memory, but her mind was miles away. Why was Kent Calvert carrying so much cash? Was he planning a long trip? Where was he going on a stormy night? What was the motive for the shooting? Try as she might, Noelle couldn't concentrate on the minister's sermon.

As the service finally ended, the organist played the postlude. The congregation began filing out of the wooden pews. Noelle's siblings clamored off to get a free doughnut served downstairs in the fellowship hall, the fancy name of the large finished basement. Her parents chatted with the couple in the pew behind them. Noelle gave her folks a brief goodbye and pushed her way past the people heading toward the exit. If she hurried, she'd have time to stop by the hospital before donning her witch's costume for the afternoon shows. But Gus E. Monty—he insisted on using his middle initial—one of her former schoolmates, intercepted her. He stretched his arm across the doorway into the narthex and rested his hand on the frame, blocking her way. As usual, he stood out in the crowd in his red tie and checkered jacket

"Hello, Noelle." With his white teeth and charming dimples, he should have been a teen idol instead of a local nuisance. "We missed you in Sunday School this morning."

"I missed me too. I slept in."

"You were busy last night?" He waggled his eyebrows suggestively.

"You could say that."

"Who was he?"

Her stomach knotted. How did he know about her visitor? "Who?"

"Your date last night. If you were busy on a Saturday night, you must have been on a date."

She crossed her arms. How could she have a romantic life in dullsville? The boys she grew up with who remained in town were immature or obnoxious; the decent ones had found jobs elsewhere. Most of her male school chums had long since married, leaving Yuletide with a short supply of bachelors, including Gus.

"No, I wasn't on a date," she said.

"Did you get caught in that storm last night? That was a dilly. I was driving back from an insurance seminar in Indy. Almost got washed off the road."

What a shame he wasn't. "I'm glad you got home all right."

Gus moved to let another person out of the sanctuary, but before Noelle could escape, he barred her with his other arm. "Speaking of dates, what are you doing next Saturday night?"

"Same thing I do every Saturday night. Working at the park."

"How about Friday night? We can go to the high school game. The Elves are playing in town. When we were in school you used to love screaming your head off during the basketball games."

"Working."

"Don't you do anything besides work?"

"Sleeping."

"Monday, then."

"Dinner with my parents. And speaking of work, you'll have to excuse me. I really have to go." She half-closed her eyes and put on a wicked grin. "It's time for me to get witchy."

Noelle ducked under his arm and hurried to the Beetle. She could have made herself available on Monday, but the regular weekly supper with her family provided a convenient excuse for avoiding people like Gus. His only interest in her was due to his parents' insistence that he settle down, and Noelle was one of the few spinsters in town. Most Yuletide girls picked up a wedding ring shortly after receiving their high school diplomas.

Noelle drove the Bug straight to St. Nicholas Hospital. To keep her gloves clean, she left them in the car's glove box. At the admitting desk, she asked to see Kent Calvert.

The nurse, looking efficient with her hair pinned up beneath a starched white cap, and clad in a white dress, pantyhose and flat shoes, consulted the register book. "I'm sorry, but there's nobody here by that name."

Had the ambulance taken the man to another city? "I'm sure he was brought here last night. Young man, dark hair, black leather jacket. I think he had a gunshot wound in his chest."

"Gunshot?" Another look at the book. "Do you mean the John Doe? We had a patient admitted last night who had no identification."

"I guess the guys in the ambulance didn't know his name. Can I see him? I want to return his wallet."

"I'm afraid that isn't possible."

"Did he check out? Is he still unconscious?"

"I'm sorry, Miss McNabb. He's dead."

Chapter 4: Dr. Robert

Noelle didn't expect that answer. "Are you sure?"

"Yes, Miss McNabb." The nurse pursed her lips. "We make certain of things like that."

"What happened? Didn't the doctors try to help him? Did they try surgery or—"

"I wasn't on duty last night so I can't say for certain what happened, but our patients receive the highest quality of care."

From the stories she'd heard around town, Noelle doubted that statement, but she let it slide. "Where is he now?"

"Obviously he is no longer here. Once a patient expires, the deceased is transported out of the hospital as quickly as possible."

"Was he taken to one of the local funeral homes?"

"What is your interest in the John Doe? Are you a member of the family?"

"No, I—" How could she describe her relationship with the stranger? "Does anyone know who shot him?"

The nurse squared her shoulders and her voice grew cold. "You would need to talk to the police about that. This is a hospital, not a detective agency."

"Did any of his family show up? Who claimed the body?"

"I'm afraid I can't answer any more questions. Patient information is confidential."

"Confidential? Are you kidding? I've heard Doc Robert at church chattering away about his cases."

The nurse lowered her head and began shuffling

some manila patient folders on the counter. "You'll have to excuse me, Miss McNabb. I'm very busy."

"Is there someone else I can talk to?"

The nurse sat in an armless chair and swiveled around with her back to the counter. She picked up the phone and began dialing. Was she warning the hospital administrator about this nosy person, or just pretending to place a call to avoid further questions? Noelle trudged to the lobby exit door, but stopped halfway. She glanced over her shoulder and, when the nurse wasn't looking, she ducked down a white-walled hallway. Noelle had been in the hospital when her mother gave birth to the twins and her dad had heart problems, so she knew the layout. If anyone asked, Noelle would say she was here to see a patient during visiting hours. A couple of nurses and an orderly in white pants and a tunic passed her, oblivious of her presence. St. Nicholas was a quiet place that dealt with the aches and pains of kids growing up and adults getting older, but had never handled a murder case.

At the end of the first-floor hallway, Noelle barged into the wood-paneled outer office of the hospital administrator. This being Sunday, the executive secretary was not here, but sometimes the chief doctor came in on weekends to catch up on his paperwork. Noelle bypassed the empty secretarial desk and stormed straight into the inner office.

The chief administrator of St. Nicholas, a middle-aged man with a trimmed moustache and salt-and-pepper hair, glanced up from the papers on his desk and set down his fountain pen. "Noelle. This is unexpected."

"Sorry to bother you, doc, but the nurse at the admitting desk is giving me the runaround."

The leather in the executive chair creaked as Doctor Robert shifted his position, leaning back slightly. "I find that hard to believe. Our staff prides itself on diligence and care. Are you trying to get a room for yourself? You don't look ill."

"I'm trying to get some information about a patient. A man was brought in last night in the ambulance. He had been shot."

Doctor Robert set his lips firmly together and cleared his throat. He steepled his fingers. "You mean the John Doe? How do you know about him?"

"Because the ambulance picked him up from my living room. He walked into my house last night and collapsed."

"How does he concern you?"

"He was murdered. Not by me, of course. But I'd like to find where he is now."

"Nobody said he was murdered."

"He had blood all over his shirt."

"Perhaps he was suffering from a nosebleed."

The corners of Noelle's mouth turned down even more. "People don't die of nosebleeds. Which funeral home has him?"

"I really can't say. The body was taken out of town."

"Taken by whom? Did someone claim the body? Or did you just stick poor Mr. Calvert in a taxi and tell the driver to go anywhere he pleased?"

The doctor rose to his feet. "We treat all of our patients with the utmost dignity and care. I assure you, everything was handled in the proper manner. That's all I can say, Noelle. I must ask you to leave and not bother anyone else about this matter."

"I wasn't trying to pry. I just don't see what's wrong about finding out what happened to a guy who almost died inside my house."

His finger hovered over a switch on the desk's intercom. "Do I need to call someone to give you an escort out?"

"No. I just want to know what's the big secret."

The doctor gave her a condescending smile. "There's no secret at all. A patient dies and is moved on. Happens all the time. That's all, Noelle. You can go now."

The doctor's voice had a tone of finality. He wasn't going to give any answers, no matter how much she pleaded. Rather than having a security guard force her out, Noelle turned to leave.

"Have a nice day," he said.

Noelle glanced back over her shoulder and shot him a sour look. "Yeah, right."

As she drove to the park, she rolled down the window so she could breathe the rain-washed air. With the patient labeled as a John Doe, was the body shipped to the county morgue, the final resting place for transients found by the railroad tracks? If so, why didn't the doctor tell her? What was the big mystery? As much as she yearned to drive to the morgue and find out, Noelle had a show to do and she was already late. After parking the Bug at the theme park, she ran to the dressing room, dodging the clusters of tourists. The sun was drying up the rain puddles, and a mass of tourists crowded the park. Maybe she'd have some attentive audiences today.

The stage manager, dressed in a polo shirt, pants and a windbreaker, was waiting for her in front of the dressing room. "There you are! I was ready to call in a replacement."

Noelle glared at him. "I never miss a show. You know that. Now will you please move so I can go inside and dress?"

The stage manager stepped aside and Noelle rushed inside. She tossed her purse and hat into her locker as the elves began filing out for their entrance. Noelle threw on her costume, almost putting it on backwards in her haste. She sighed and straightened the long dress. She slapped on the green makeup while the show's opening music drifted through the loudspeaker on the wall. She'd have to put on the eyebrows after the first show. As she ran up the back stairs, Noelle tried to secure the witch's hat on her head, jabbing the long pin into her scalp instead of her hair. Ouch! In her haste she tripped over the dress hem. She reached out a hand and grabbed the back wall to keep from falling. She reached the wings just as one of the elves spoke her cue. Noelle paused long enough to suck in a deep breath and calm her thoughts before rushing on stage. She channeled her frustration at the hospital staff into her performance, shouting her lines with a wickedness that nearly had the kids in the front row in tears.

Backstage after the show, Rudolph removed his deer head. "What's with you today? I thought you were going to bite off my head. Are you on the rag?"

"No, not that it's any of your business," Noelle said.

The stage manager walked up and patted her on the arm. "Keep up the energy, Noelle. I liked what you did today."

Noelle stuck out her tongue at Rudolph and walked away. The kids in the cast were so boring. As the deer ran off to flirt with the young does downstairs, Noelle realized she'd missed lunch. Park rules said performers in costume were not allowed to roam the park as not to spoil the illusion for the guests. Noelle found the sound guy, the kid who sat backstage and ran the tape machine with the pre-recorded instrumental music for the elves' songs. She gave him two quarters and asked him to fetch some food from one of the park's restaurants. The young guy returned shortly with a paper-wrapped Penguin Patty (hamburger), paper pouch of Santa Spuds (French fries) and a paper cup of A&W, the only brand of root beer carried at the park.

At the end of the shift, Noelle drove home relaxed because she was finished with the witch's role until Friday evening. During the months when the park was only open weekends, Noelle had a second job during the week that was far less demanding than acting. At home, Noelle fed Ceebee and then popped a Swanson frozen dinner into the oven. By Sunday night the fridge was sparse and, besides, she didn't feel like cooking. While supper was heating up, she changed into her jammies, relieved to get out of the tights. Dinner consisted of fried shrimp, peas and crinkle-cut potatoes set in the three compartments of the foil tray. Her favorite weather girl took a break on Sundays, so Noelle skipped the TV news. After a quick cleanup of the kitchen, she took a glass of milk and a saucer of cookies into the living room to lounge on the sofa and enjoy the many sections of the Sunday newspaper. Ceebee curled up beside her to wash his face and belly. Before hitting the comics, Noelle scanned the main news for anything about Kent Calvert. Nothing. A man was murdered and no one noticed? Maybe an obituary would show up in a few days. She picked up the scissors to clip out the coupons when the phone rang.

She didn't recognize the man's voice on the other end of the line. "Where is it?" he demanded without so much as a 'hello.'

"Who is this?" Noelle spoke firmly. As the recipient of crank calls over the years, pranksters didn't intimidate her.

"That doesn't matter. We need you to turn it over immediately."

"What is 'it'?" She expected to hear a lewd punch line in return.

"We know you have it." The man was straightforward and serious.

"Who are you? Who are 'we'? Is this a joke?"

"No, ma'am. The nation's security depends on you handing it over."

She hung up. She was too tired to play twenty questions with an anonymous man. The phone rang again—probably the same creep calling back. On the tenth ring she unplugged the phone line from the wall jack for some peace and quiet. Did the caller want Kent's money? But nobody knew the man had been at her house except for the hospital staff and the police, and even they did not know about the cash. Out of curiosity, she removed Kent's wallet from her purse and inspected the billfold for hidden compartments, but she found nothing unusual. She hid the wallet behind a fat dictionary in the bookshelf, and decided the caller had the wrong number. But as Noelle tried to read *Peanuts*, she couldn't keep her mind off the murdered stranger.

Chapter 5: Your Mother Should Know
Monday

Noelle's weekday job at the Groovy Vinyl Record Store gave her the inside scoop on rock and roll and the first chance to listen to the new releases from The Beatles, The Who and the Rolling Stones, the kind of music that drove her parents crazy. The downside of the job was dealing with the silly schoolgirls going gaga over Davy Jones and Lesley Gore.

Since her work involved bending and lifting heavy boxes, the manger let her wear pants on the job. Today she wore tan slacks, flats and a floral print cardigan buttoned over a blouse. Mondays started out slow, so Noelle used the down time to organize the records sitting in the rows of bins, as customers often glanced at the album covers and stuck them back in the wrong spot. She set up a display of cardboard record covers in the front window, after first removing the vinyl to avoid warping the discs in the sun. The record listening booths needed dusting and a check to see if the hi-fi needles required replacement.

Near the front door stood the checkout counter and a brass register with keys inlaid with mother-of-pearl. The back wall had two doorways: one leading to the office and storage room, and the other to the head shop. A beaded curtain over the doorway hid the head shop from the general public. A small sign on the wall stated that minors could not enter the room. The operation had nothing to do with the record store. Noelle never entered the room or rang up the head shop sales.

Noelle set a cardboard box on the counter and opened it. She removed a record and read the cover liner notes. After tearing off the plastic wrapping, she placed the disc on the turntable and pressed "play." The needle dropped in place. The song "Born Free" boomed over the wall speakers as Santa Claus entered the shop. He wasn't the real Kris Kringle, of course—he only portrayed the jolly old man at the theme park. Christopher Kloss also served as the town's part-time mayor. A jacket covered his white shirt, dark pants and red suspenders.

"Morning, Chris, what can I do for you?" Noelle nodded at the turntable. "That's the brand new Andy Williams album. Like it?" She knew the tastes of the regular customers.

"Hello, Noelle. I'll give it a listen later." The large man sported a full white beard, ruddy cheeks and a huge tummy, but today he lacked the usual twinkle in his blue eyes. "I hear you've been bothering people over at the hospital."

"News travels fast around here." She leaned her elbows on the counter. "Do you mean yesterday? I was checking up on a patient who seems to have mysteriously disappeared."

"There's no need to worry your pretty little head about it."

She bristled, not only at the way he talked down to her but how nobody treated the late Kent Calvert as a real person. "A man was murdered. Why isn't Chief Whitlock trying to find the killer? Or would that take him away from his five-hour lunch breaks at The Igloo?" The downtown pharmacy/soda fountain was built to resemble a domed icehouse.

"That's the point, Noelle. News of a shooting might be bad business for Yuletide. When you think of Christmas, you don't want to link it to murder. As the mayor, I need to look out for the community welfare. We don't want a suspicious death to chase away the tourists now, do we? If the park closes, many of our fine citizens would lose their jobs, including you and me."

Might not be a big loss if that stupid park went out of business, she thought. "Sounds more like the spirit of Scrooge and his money. Don't you feel we owe this stranger some justice?"

"I do, I do. But the police are conducting a quiet investigation. No point in getting people riled up. Noelle, I'm asking you as a friend, don't spread this around town. We don't want a bunch of silly rumors floating around, now do we?"

"No, you don't."

"Promise me you'll keep this under your hat?"

The bell over the front door jingled as a family of four entered the shop. Saved by the bell. Since the local kids were in school at this hour, they must be tourists.

"If you'll excuse me, Chris, I have customers."

Before he could object, she slipped from behind the counter and approached the family to ask if they needed assistance. They were traveling through on their way to Ohio for a family funeral and wanted to find a good restaurant where they could eat and freshen up. Noelle cheerfully gave directions to the North Pole Café, the town's only sit-down restaurant not inside the theme park. By the time she finished with the family, Kloss had left. That suited Noelle, as she had no intention of making promises she couldn't keep. Business in the store picked up until noon when the customers had left and the proprietor of the head shop finally drifted in. Noelle wondered how he managed to stay in business since he never kept regular hours, only showing up as the mood struck.

"Hi, Rambler," she said. "What's happening?"

"Hey, baby, I'm totally bummed." He spoke in a low, raspy voice.

The tall, lanky dude looked out of place anywhere else in Yuletide except here. A bandana was tied around his stringy, shoulder-length blond hair. He wore a fringed leather vest over a long-sleeved tie-dye shirt as well as patched and faded blue jeans and leather sandals, chilly for the spring weather. Over one shoulder hung a leather bag, no doubt holding new merchandise to sell. Noelle took a sniff and realized the man hadn't bathed recently.

"That's too bad. Where's Moonbaby?"

He scratched his long beard. "My old lady's at the farm. One of the goats butted a hole in the fence and she's getting it fixed."

"Which, the fence or the goat?"

He laughed with a deep, throaty chortle. Most of the residents shunned the longhaired weirdo, but Noelle like the kook despite his appearance. He possessed a warped sense of humor much like her own, and was a nonconformist to boot. In return for Noelle befriending the oddballs, they often shared their farm produce with her.

The record store manager arrived to take over for the rest of the day. But before she left, Noelle wanted to chat with the hippie.

"Rambler, I'm off work now. Want to join me for lunch?"

"I'm busted, man. All out of bread."

"I brought lunch. I'll share."

Noelle took the hippie into the back workroom where she had stored her sack lunch and thermos of grape juice. They sat across from each other at the small table in the center of the room. Plastic milk crates full of albums and metal file cabinets stuffed with paper sales records lined the walls. Noelle opened her brown paper bag and handed Rambler a neatly cut half of a baloney sandwich covered with Saran wrap. She tore open the bag of Fritos and unwrapped the foil around the carrot and celery sticks. Fortunately, she'd brought two Twinkies instead of the usual one. Noelle gave her companion one of the snack cakes.

"Help yourself to the chips and vegetables. Sorry I can't give you any grape juice, but I only brought one cup."

"Hey, no sweat. I got a cooler full of Cokes in the shop." He gobbled his sandwich.

"Rambler, I got a problem, but you can't breathe a word of this to anyone except Moonbaby."

"I can dig it."

As they ate, Noelle told him about Kent Calvert, the hospital staff and the mayor. She felt safe sharing her secrets with the hippies, as they were experts at keeping their own affairs hush-hush in the community. Besides, if they did talk, most people would dismiss their babblings as the ravings of an acid trip.

As the end of the story, Rambler looked shocked. "Whoa, you're laying down some heavy stuff."

"What do you mean?"

Rambler leaned in and whispered. "That dude who checked out of this life, I knew him."

Noelle blinked with astonishment. "Kent Calvert? You couldn't possibly know him. He didn't live around here."

"Didn't say I knew him well. But last Saturday he hitched a ride with me and the woman back from Riverbend."

So that's how Kent arrived in town. "But he wasn't shot when you picked him up, was he?"

"No way, man. We'd of patched him up if he was. When the kid left us, he was all right and outta sight."

The manager entered the room to retrieve some

papers from a file cabinet. Noelle didn't want her boss to overhear their conversation.

"Come on, Rambler, let's beat it."

They'd polished off the food, so she tossed the paper bag and crumpled foil into a wastebasket and capped the thermos. She put on her coat and, with purse and thermos in hand, left the room with Rambler.

She said to him, "We need to talk about this, but somewhere private."

"Yeah, no sweat. Drop in at the farm anytime. My woman loves company. She says she get lonely with nobody around but the chickens and the goats and me, the old goat."

"I'm busy today, but how about tomorrow?"

Rambler gave a vague "yeah." Time was flexible for the hippies, who rarely consulted a clock or calendar. He slipped through the beaded curtain into the dark head shop. Noelle left the store through a back door for the sun-lit parking lot behind the building. She hopped into the Beetle and ran errands. She returned a library book, paid bills, and filled the gas tank. At the grocery store she deposited some empty Frostie bottles for the refund. When she finished shopping, the bag boy loaded the paper bags stuffed with food into the VW's front trunk and she headed home.

The cat met her on the porch with a mouse in his mouth. "Ceebee! Look at you! You little mouser." She spoke affectionately. She appreciated his efforts at rodent control. But then Ceebee tried to nudge his way into the cottage.

"You are not bringing that thing into the house!" Her arms were loaded with grocery bags, so she gently pushed the cat out of the way with her foot. "Move! I have to put away the food before it spoils and then I'll tend to you."

After unlocking the door and squeezing past the cat,

Noelle put away her purchases while Ceebee amused himself outside with the mouse. After he'd devoured the snack, she let him inside. The cat ran into the kitchen, jumped on a chair, put his front paws on the back of the chair, and stared at the cabinet holding the cat food.

"You just ate a mouse! How can you possibly be hungry again?"

Mindful of the animal's bottomless stomach, Noelle poured him a small bowl of food. As he munched, she filled a cup with water and sat at the table. With the water and a finger she moistened the back of the green stamps she had earned with her grocery store purchase and pasted the squares into a booklet. Only a few more pages to fill and she could redeem the booklet for a prize. When finished with the stamps, she put away the bowl and booklet, and glanced at the Felix The Cat clock. Time to head out to her parents' house. On Monday nights she dropped in back home for a good home-cooked meal, the latest news and a sack full of food and household goods from a mother who still felt her child couldn't survive on her own. Noelle let Ceebee outside and drove back into town to Reindeer Road, a residential street of well-kept, two-story homes with large, neatly mowed front lawns. She pulled into one side of the driveway so her dad could park his Chevy in the garage. Noelle took the front steps two at a time and pushed opened the front door. When the McNabbs were home they didn't lock the doors.

"Hi mom, where are you?"

"Is that you, Noelle? I'm in the kitchen."

The daughter's mouth watered at the aroma of meatloaf, boiled potatoes and veggies—green beans and corn fresh from last summer when Mrs. McNabb canned them in glass jars. Noelle had the good luck to miss liver-and-onions night. Despite the cool temperature outside, the busy kitchen was warm. Mom had an apron tied over her housedress. Her nylon stockings were rolled down to the tops of her canvas sneakers. As usual, her gray hair was set in tight perm curls held in place with hairspray.

"Hi, sweetie," Mom said. "Help me mash the potatoes? You always liked doing that."

The daughter barely had time to set her purse on the kitchen table and take off her jacket before Mom shoved a metal masher and a pan of still-warm potatoes into her hands. Mom was raised on the creed of hard work with never an idle moment, so the women talked while they cooked. Noelle placed the hot pan atop a fabric hot pad on the table and added milk, butter, parsley and garlic to the spuds before she began mashing.

"You got your hair cut," Mom said. "I noticed it yesterday, but you ran out after church before we could talk."

"Sorry to scoot, but I had to get to work. I had my hair done at a salon in Riverbend. Do you like it?"

"You have such pretty hair. Seems a shame to get rid of it."

"There's still plenty left. But the shorter hair is easier to handle. I always had to pin it up when I put on my costume. Now I can just pop the wig on and off with less fuss."

"Why didn't you go to the beautician here in town? All my friends and I use Cecilia."

"You mean the woman at Mrs. Claus' Beauty Shop? She's all right, but she doesn't know the new styles."

"I don't know why you youngsters have to change everything just to change it. Did you know Julia Beems is engaged?"

Noelle bit her lip. She knew where this topic was headed. "No, I didn't."

"You were friends with her in school. I though she'd ask you to be one of her bridesmaids."

"No, she didn't. We were never that close."

"I saw you talking with Gus at church yesterday."

Noelle rolled her eyes. "Oh, him. He was talking to me, not the other way around."

"What did he want?"

The daughter resisted the temptation to say, "He wants to jump my bones," and instead said, "Nothing important. He just wants to go out with me."

"Why don't you?"

"Mom, he's a creep."

"You don't know that until you get to know him better."

Noelle sighed. Talks like this reminded her of the teasing she endured in college as being one of the few girls who was more interested in learning the craft and getting a B.A. than in landing a husband as a M.R.S.

"I just don't want to get involved in anyone right now," Noelle said. "Maybe later."

"You know what they say. Missies who wait too late, miss out."

"If I was looking for a guy, I could do a lot better than Gus. I want to get out in the world, Mom. See if anything exists beyond the border of Yuletide."

"This isn't such a bad little town. It's much better than Riverbend. Safe streets, friendly people, no crime."

Noelle coughed loudly and whacked the defenseless potatoes even harder. A man was murdered near her cottage, and the townsfolk were giving her the cold shoulder. Safe and friendly, indeed.

"What's the matter, sweetie?" Mom asked. "Is something bothering you? You don't sound as chipper as usual."

Noelle was dying to tell Mom about Kent Calvert.

Her mother usually gave her good advice or at least a shoulder to cry on. But she held back. Would Mom blab her confidence to her friends in the Monday morning women's Bible study or the Peppermint Angels, the women's service and philanthropic group? Chances are, Mom would hear about it soon enough from the other ladies. When the old biddies started gabbing over their coffee and doughnuts, secrets spread as quickly as the winter flu outbreaks at the schools. Besides, Noelle didn't know enough about the situation to explain it.

"I'm just tired, I guess," said the daughter. "I need to get away. Get out of the rut I'm in. See something besides the same old buildings and the same old people. I want to live a little before I'm tied down with kids and all."

"Don't you listen to those foolish women's libbers. They're just shriveled up old prunes because they don't have families of their own. Raising children is the best thing a woman can do." She wrapped an arm around her daughter's waist and squeezed. "I'm glad I had you."

Noelle smiled. "I am too."

"Besides, I'd like to play with my grandchildren before I'm an old woman."

Another fierce pounding on the taters.

"Noelle, I think those potatoes are ready. You don't need to poke a hole in the bottom of the pan."

Before she could reply, her eight-year-old brother, wearing a strange outfit, entered the kitchen.

"Donny!" Noelle exclaimed. "What on earth happened to your ears?"

Chapter 6: Little Children

Donny wore a long-sleeved tunic of blue velvet. His black pants were tucked into the tops of his black knee boots. His eyebrows arched upward, thanks to the eyebrow pencil he had snitched from Mom's dresser. Oddly, the tips of his ears were pointed, not round.

He spoke in a monotone. "I am Mr. Spock, first science officer of the USS Enterprise. My five-year mission is to explore strange new worlds—"

Mom interrupted. "Your mission, young man, is to wash your hands and call your sister downstairs for supper. It's time to eat."

Donny eyed his older sibling. He pulled a homemade cardboard gun from his belt and pointed it at her. "A hideous Klingon! Fire phasers!" He made the "zapping" noise of an imaginary phaser beam.

Noelle clawed her nails at him and growled. "I am a Martian monster and I'm going to eat you up!" Honestly, kid brothers could be so annoying.

"Phasers are not functioning! Fire photon torpedoes!"

Mom lightly slapped her son on the rump. "Go and wash up, now."

"Beam me up, Scotty." With that exit line, the boy ran into the downstairs bathroom, the only washroom in the house.

"He's certainly fond of *Star Trek*," Noelle said.

Mom shrugged as she removed the pans of vegetables from the stovetop. "We let him watch it. It seems harmless enough. In a year or two he'll forget all about that silly show."

"How did he make the pointed ears?"

"Play-Doh."

A familiar baritone voice wafted in from the foyer. "Honey, I'm home!"

Mom rushed about the kitchen. "Hurry and set the table, dear. Your father's here."

Noelle grabbed the cloth placemats and napkins and the plastic plates from the drawers and cabinets. She set the places at the dining room table. The furniture in the room consisted of a table made of chrome tube legs and a colored Formica top. The matching chairs had the same chrome legs along with padded seats and backs that matched the tabletop's color.

When the kid brother stepped out of the bathroom, Mom said, "Donny, change your clothes. No aliens at the table."

"That is illogical," replied Donny, but seeing his mother's stern look, he hurried upstairs.

Dad set his metal lunch box and thermos on the kitchen counter for washing. He loosened the tie that hung over his starched white shirt. He and Mom shared a quick kiss.

"How was your day?" he asked.

"Busy as usual. Mabel said there's been some problems at the plant," Mom said.

Dad looked startled. "What sort of problems?"

"Something about drawings and files disappearing."

"I don't know where she'd hear a story like that. We keep all of our confidential papers under lock and key." He laughed. "You know Mabel. She isn't happy unless she's spreading some kind of silly gossip." Dad hugged Noelle. "And how's my favorite girl?"

"Just fine, Dad." She wasn't fine, but love from Dad made her forget her anxieties for a moment.

Dad kept his arms around Noelle's waist but leaned

back to eye his daughter. "You seem upset about something."

"It's nothing. I just need a rest."

"I should think so, working two jobs. Why don't you take some time off? The family vacation is coming up in July. Where would you like to go this year?"

"Can we do something besides camp at a state park? We've seen every tree there is to see. I've been bitten by every mosquito in the world."

Her mother said, "How about Cedar Point in Cincinnati? The twins have been pestering me about going there."

"Mom, I work at an amusement park. I don't need to spend two weeks looking at another one."

Dad said, "If we go to Cedar Point, you could put in an application to work at one of the shows there. That might be something different that what you're doing now."

"I'd rather get a acting job in Hollywood."

"I don't know about that," Dad said. "Los Angeles is a pretty scary place for a young lady. All that crime and smog."

The oven timer dinged. "Noelle, help me with the food, please," said Mom.

Dad went to wash his hands in the bathroom and then put his tie away in the downstairs bedroom. Mom put on an oven mitt and removed a pan of sizzling meatloaf from the oven. Slabs of bacon and lines of ketchup criss-crossed the mound of seasoned ground beef. With a metal spatula, Mom slid the meatloaf onto a serving plate. Noelle drained the green beans and corn and poured the veggies into separate bowls. The well-mashed taters went into their own dish as well. The women placed the various dishes on hot plates set on the dining room table. Noelle poured glasses of milk for her siblings, and placed the coffee pot on a footed metal stand for the adults. Mom removed her apron and left it in the kitchen.

The twins, Dolly and Donny, clopped downstairs. She was in a blouse and overalls, and he was now in regular pants and shirt. They plopped onto their chairs, nearly sliding off the slick plastic coating on the chair seats.

When Dad entered the dining room, he said to Donny, "Ears!"

The boy frowned. He yanked the clay tips off his ear tops and stuck them in his pocket.

The parents took their places at the ends of the table. The older daughter sat on the side opposite the two brats. When Dolly began whining, Noelle remembered why she preferred living alone.

"Mom!" Dolly said. "It's almost time for *The Monkees.*"

Mom glanced at the sunburst wall clock. "Your show doesn't start until six-thirty. We have plenty of time."

Donny chimed in, "How come she gets to watch her stupid show every week and I haffa miss *Gilligan's Island?*"

"She doesn't see it every week," Mom replied. "You know the rule. She watches her program one week, and you see yours the next. What you missed you can catch in summer reruns."

Donny continued unabated. "My friend Ernie, his folks have two TVs in their house."

Dad laid a napkin across his lap. "We don't need two television sets. If you're bored, you can go outside and play in the yard. Now let's say grace before the food gets cold."

The family members bowed their heads and folded their hands. As dad recited the table grace, Noelle peeked and saw Donny punch Dolly's arm. She slapped him back. After the "amen," they all passed the serving dishes and spooned big helpings onto their plates. Noelle grabbed the woven breadbasket and unwrapped the cloth covering the warm Pillsbury dinner rolls. She tore apart a roll and cut a pat of butter from the butter plate. She slathered the roll with butter and bit into the light brown flaky crust. She loved these easy-to-make biscuits, but any rolls baked at her place ended up charred. As a kid, Noelle had no interest in homemaking, but now that she lived on her own she realized she should have paid more attention during the home ec cooking classes.

Dad asked the twins about their day at school and discussed some housekeeping items with Mom. Noelle gobbled the tasty food. The kids picked on each other.

During a lull in the conversation, Noelle asked, "How are things at the plant, Dad?"

"Busy," he said. "NASA's gearing up with the space program, and we're swamped with new components."

"Really? What are they like?"

"'Fraid I can't tell you that. It's top secret."

"How can anyone keep a secret in this town? The employees know about it, don't they?"

"Just the upper management. We dole out the components so the technicians only work on one piece at a time. They don't see the entire package."

"Mom! It's almost time for my show! I'm missing Davy!" Dolly fidgeted as if she needed to use the bathroom.

Mom didn't look up as she speared a hunk of meatloaf with her fork. "The show isn't on for ten minutes. You don't need to turn on the set so early."

"I gotta give the TV time to warm up!"

After the family demolished the food, Mom brought out a freshly baked apple pie and a paper carton of vanilla ice cream. With a metal pie cutter she deftly sliced the pie and slipped each wedge onto a dessert place. Dad topped each treat with a scoop of ice cream. Noelle attacked her ice cream before the hot pie melted it.

"Can I eat this in the living room while I watch TV?" Dolly asked.

"No. I don't want you spilling food on the floor," Mom replied.

The grandfather clock in the living room bonged the half-hour.

"My show's starting!" the girl shouted.

"No, it isn't," said Mom. "You know that clock runs fast."

Dolly shoved half the pie slice into her mouth at once while staring at the wall clock, as if mentally trying to slow it down.

"And chew your food. Don't gulp it," Mom continued.

Donny grinned. "That's one way to shut her up."

The girl was too busy choking down her dessert to make a rebuttal. "Okay, I'm done now. Can I be excused, please, please, please?"

Before waiting for a reply, Dolly scrapped back her chair and dashed into the living room. Seconds later, the catchy *Monkees* theme song drowned out the table conversation.

"And turn it down!" Mom yelled. The TV volume subsided a little. She shook her head. "Kids nowadays. What does she see in that Davy Jones kid anyway?"

Dad said, "Seems to me when you were her age, you had a crush on Frank Sinatra."

"That's different. Frankie has class."

After the desserts were consumed, the family scattered. Donny fled upstairs to his room. Since Dolly had the TV on in the living room, Dad retired to the den—actually a cluster of chairs and tables in one corner of the finished basement—to read the newspaper in peace. Noelle helped her mother carry the dishes to the kitchen for the post-meal cleanup routine. After packing up the leftovers, Mom put on her apron and filled the sink with soapy water for washing. Noelle found a clean dishtowel for drying the dishes. As they worked, Mom shared the latest town news until Dolly's TV program had finished and she ran upstairs to play her *More of the Monkees* record at full blast.

"Noelle, will please you tell your sister to close her door when she listens to her music?" said Mom.

The daughter set down the dishtowel and dutifully ran up the stairs, two at a time. She stuck her head into her kid sister's room as the song "She" blasted from the tinny-sounding speakers on the portable turntable atop the dresser. The bedroom walls were plastered with pages of Monkees photos torn from teen magazines.

"Mom said you have to shut your door when you play your racket."

Dolly sat on the bed, facing the spinning disc. She glanced over her shoulder at her sib. "It is not racket."

Noelle closed the bedroom door herself and peeked into Donny's room. Star maps covered the walls. Models of plastic spaceships put together from kits hung from the ceiling. The boy sat on the twin bed and leaned against the headboard, knees drawn up, reading *Tom Swift and the Subocean Geotron*. Noelle wasn't sure if he'd grow up to be an astronaut, a science fiction writer, or just a nut watching nothing but sci-fi shows. She headed downstairs.

Her parents were seated on the living room sofa watching *I Dream of Jeannie*. Mom invited Noelle to join them, but the daughter bid good night instead. The antics of an astronaut and his genie seemed insignificant compared to the mystery of Kent Calvert. Mom got up and provided her daughter with a sack of cookies and canned jars of homemade sweet pickles, applesauce and green beans. During the drive home, Noelle wondered where she could go to find some answers about Kent. She could track down the address on his driver's license and talk to his family as well as confront Chief Whitlock about his investigation— assuming he'd even started poking around.

Halfway down the driveway to the cottage, she stopped the car. A black, four-door sedan was parked in front of the garage. Nobody she knew owned a car like that. The tinted windows blocked any view of the driver. She hoped the auto didn't contain another dead or dying man. If bodies kept piling up at her house, Whitlock would get suspicious. Noelle switched off the headlights and engine, got out and rapped on the driver's side window of the sedan. The glass lowered halfway. The driver, a man around thirty-five, had on sunglasses. Dark glasses at dusk?

"Excuse me," she said, "but you're blocking my driveway."

"You're Noelle McNabb, correct?" He spoke in a calm, businesslike manner, not hostile but certainly not friendly.

"Yeah, who are you?"

"We need to talk."

"I recognize your voice. You're the crank who called me last night. What was that all about?"

"That's what we need to talk about."

"No, we don't. You need to get out of my yard."

"I must insist."

The man rolled up the window and opened the door, pushing Noelle back. She recovered her footing as he stepped out of the vehicle. The lean, fit man towered over her by a couple of inches. His dark hair was in a buzz cut. As he buttoned his black suit jacket, she caught a glimpse of a shoulder holster filled with a gun.

"Yeah," she said. "I guess we should talk."

Chapter 7: Secret Agent Man

"But not here." The man swiveled his head from side to side, as if looking for something. Noelle couldn't guess his intentions with the dark glasses hiding his eyes. "Listening devices can pick up our voices. We need to go inside."

"What? Inside my house?"

"Yes, that's the nearest building."

"You expect me to let a strange man into my house?"

"I'm not strange. I'm really quite ordinary."

"Ordinary people don't drive in the dark with their sunglasses on."

A light mist began to fall, but the coatless man didn't seem to notice. He simply stood with his face toward her as if staring her down. Noelle shivered in the cool air. Despite the man's secretive manner, she didn't fear him. After all, he hadn't pulled out his gun—yet. She was tired from her busy day and wanted to warm up inside the house. The quicker the man had his say, the sooner he'd be gone and she could relax.

"Okay," she said. "Let me get my keys."

Noelle dug the keys out of her purse, and he followed her to the porch. As she unlocked the front door, Ceebee came bouncing in from the woods but stopped short. He stared at the man and hissed.

"Ceebee, stop that. He's okay."

The feline growled.

She looked at the man. "I'm sorry, that's my cat. He takes a while to warm up to strangers."

"So I see. Does he bite?"

"No, just makes a lot of noise. Ceebee, settle down."

She pushed the door open. The cat slipped between Noelle's legs, almost tripping her, and ran inside to duck beneath the couch.

"Come in. I haven't had a chance to clean. I wasn't expecting company." She closed the door behind them and turned on the overhead light and the thermostat. "Have a seat. Umm, want some coffee or something? A soda?"

He remained standing. "No, thank you." The man removed his sunglasses, revealing brown eyes that took in the room without blinking. The lean face reminded her of a hawk.

"I'm going to get something for myself," she said. "I'm really thirsty."

"Yes, but don't leave through the back door."

"How did you know I have a back door? You can't see it from the driveway."

"While I was waiting for your arrival, I inspected the property. Standard operating procedure. In case of emergency I need to know the location of all the exits."

Did the man have evil intentions and had checked to see how he could keep her a prisoner? She glanced at the phone on the sofa end table, the only way she could call for help.

"I did not cut your telephone line," he said, "although calling someone right now would not be a good idea."

Noelle glared at him. "Excuse me. That is, if it's all right with you."

He simply continued staring at her and made no reply. She dropped off her purse and jacket in the bedroom before heading for the kitchenette. She poured a glass of chilled, lemon-lime Kool-Aid and unlocked the back door, just in case she needed to make a quick exit. She took the glass and her sharpest carving knife into the living room.

The man was pointing a ballpoint pen at the walls. "You can set down the knife. I won't hurt you."

"If you're looking for something to write on, I can get you a piece of paper."

"What?"

She pointed the knife at his hand. "You're waving that pen around."

"This is a device to check for hidden listening devices. Bugs. We can talk. The room scopes out clean."

He replaced the pen in his shirt pocket and began to take out something else. Noelle froze. Was he going for his gun? He withdrew a black leather billfold and flipped it open for her to see a copper badge and an ID card with his photo and thumbprint.

He spoke in a matter-of-fact way. "Dash Hanover, senior control operative of the Special Intelligence Apparatus for Midwest Enemy Surveillance and Espionage."

"Siamese," she said.

"What?"

"That long bunch of words you just said. The initials spell 'Siamese.'"

He replaced the wallet inside his jacket. "Yes, a rather unfortunate acronym nobody noticed until the letterhead and ID cards had been printed."

"So are you with the CIA? FBI?"

Hanover frowned. "No. SIAMESE is a completely different agency. We operate independently from the others."

"Is it anything like UNCLE? You know, United Network Command for Law Enforcement."

"Miss McNabb, this is real life, not television fantasy. My mission here is quite serious."

"Are you a spy?"

"No. As I said, I am a control operative, not a field agent. I plan, coordinate and supervise missions but I am not an active participant. Now will you please sit down."

She did, on the sofa, and grinned. "So what does SIAMESE do? Catch the rats who are spying on us?"

Hanover perched on the edge of the recliner seat; his spine never touched the back of the chair. "You could say that. Most American intelligence efforts in regards to the Cold War are concentrated in the major cities along the East and West Coasts as well as Chicago. But recently we've seen a significant surge of activity here in the heartland. The large patches of unpopulated farmland provide excellent hiding places for enemy outposts and spies on the run. Small towns such as Yuletide contain manufacturing plants that produce goods vital to our nation's efforts in the space race. Plants such as where your father works."

"Wait a minute! How do you know where my dad works?"

"Miss McNabb, before we involve any civilians in our activities, we check them out thoroughly."

"You've been spying on me?"

"That's what we do. Will you please stop interrupting. SIAMESE was established to specifically work with counterintelligence in the central states."

"What has this to do with me?"

"Last week one of our field agents had in his possession a sixteen-millimeter filmstrip containing information vital to American interests. The agent had cut the film into three sections, with the intention of reducing each piece into a separate microdot. The data is not complete without all three sections. The agent had two microdots created and hidden before the enemy intercepted him. He managed to pass off the third piece of film to another party before he died."

Noelle perked up. "He's dead?"

"Poisoned by the enemy. But that isn't important." Hanover didn't sound emotional about the agent's death. How could he be so cold hearted? "The agent passed off the filmstrip to Kent Calvert, the young man who made his way to your house last week. We didn't locate Calvert until he was on his way to the hospital."

"So that explains the headlights I saw on the road Saturday night. You were watching my house."

"Not me. One of the field agents. Back to the point. Since you were one of the last persons to see Calvert alive, we believe he handed over the filmstrip to you for safe keeping."

She shook her head. "Sorry. The kid came in the house and fell on the floor. That's all he did. He didn't give me any film."

"What did he say to you?"

"Nothing. He just moaned a lot. Maybe the film was hidden in his clothes."

"We searched the body and found nothing."

Hanover's cold manner grated on her. "So you're the one who took him from the hospital."

"Not me personally, but another agent, yes."

"Don't you take responsibility for anything?"

"Yes, ma'am. The success or failure of this assignment falls squarely upon my shoulders."

"I hope you didn't just dump Kent's body somewhere after you got through poking around."

"Miss McNabb, we at SIAMESE are not heartless brutes. After our examination, we delivered the body to the young man's family. Now, did Calvert leave anything when he was here? A suitcase or briefcase?"

"Just a wallet. But it had nothing funky in it, just some money and cards."

Hanover held out his hand. "I need to see it."

Noelle glared at him. She hated the way this man was ordering her around in her own house. But after all, he had a gun, so she should appease him. Noelle removed the dictionary from the bookcase and pulled the wallet out of its hiding place. Once the billfold was in Hanover's hands, he removed and inspected each card and checked the leather for hidden compartments. He scrutinized the cash.

Meanwhile, Noelle returned to the sofa and sipped her Kool-Aid. "Maybe your agent gave the film to somebody else."

"Highly unlikely. Calvert picked up the film. That's a fact. The cash in the wallet was partial payment for making the drop. He was on his way to the contact point to relinquish the film and collect the remainder of his fee." He stood up. "Miss McNabb, if you do find the film, you must contact me immediately. Your country is at risk until we can successfully close this case." He took a business card from his inside jacket pocket and handed it to her. "Call this number any time, night or day. For security reasons the line does not connect directly to me. But leave a message. The operator will notify me promptly. You have an unsecured phone line, so we best not use our real names."

She smiled. "Since you're with SIAMESE, you can use the code name Litter Box."

"You think this is a joke, don't you?"

"What do you expect me to think? A guy shows up at my door half-dead, and disappears the next day. Another man with a gun shows up in my driveway and asks about a filmstrip and claims he's a spy."

"I am not a spy. I'm the senior control—"

"Yeah, I got that. It's all too weird."

Before Hanover could reply, his wristwatch beeped. He resumed his seat in the recliner, gripped the watch stem and pulled a long wire from the watchcase. He shoved the stem end into his ear; the other end of the line remained connected to the case. The operative flipped opened the watch face, revealing a tiny radio receiver, and spoke a series of nonsense syllables into the watch. When finished, he snapped shut the watch face, removed the earplug, and reeled the line back into the case. Noelle stared, dumfounded.

"Excuse me," he said. "The home office called. Since an unauthorized person was present—"

"That's me."

He nodded. "As per regulations, I used a coded message. At any rate, I must leave." Hanover moved to the door. "As far as you're concerned this meeting never occurred. You must never tell anyone that I was here or that you know about SIAMESE. Understood?"

"Yeah, yeah, I got it." Nothing would make her happier than to forget this nutty incident and get on with her life. Noelle got on her feet and opened the door for him to leave.

"And when you call," he said, "My code name is Fido Brown. You are Tabby Gray."

"What do you mean, *when*? I'm never going to—"

He slipped away without so much as a good-bye. He moved fast and apparently could see in the dark, like a cat. She considered moving the Beetle so he could back out the driveway, but Hanover deftly swung the sedan onto the lawn and around the Bug. In seconds he was on the main road.

Noelle closed the door and collapsed onto the couch. That settled that. Let the spy guy find the creep who killed Kent Calvert. With the wallet gone, she had no more attachment to the young man. She hated this cloak and dagger nonsense. The whole story of a spy hiding bits of film here and there was too bizarre. Hanover probably made it all up. Microfilms and poisons—what a load of baloney.

Just then Ceebee crawled out from under the sofa with something in his mouth.

"Ceebee, what have you got there?" Noelle reached down. "You're gonna swallow that and make yourself sick."

She tried to wrestle the item from the cat's mouth but Ceebee kept his teeth clenched. Noelle scratched the back of his neck, his favorite spot. As the cat purred, Noelle pried open his mouth and removed the item. Then she screamed.

In her hand was a five-inch strip of sixteen-millimeter film.

Chapter 8: Pictures of Matchstick Men

"Where on earth did you find this, you silly poo?"

Maybe the wallet just didn't fall out of Kent Calvert's pocket. With the cat's habit of stealing objects, maybe Ceebee had taken the billfold and the filmstrip. Noelle turned on the floor lamp and held the film up to the bulb. The miniature images on the celluloid fames were hard to see. She reached for the phone, but stopped. Why should she call Hanover right now? He was probably still in his car and would not get her message right away. She was tired and not in the mood for another visit from him tonight. Besides, she was curious as a cat. Noelle wanted to see what was on the filmstrip and why Hanover felt it was important. The chief ops could chill. She'd get back to him in her own time.

But how could she see what was on the film? She didn't have a projector—but she knew somebody who did.

Tuesday

Noelle set her Mickey Mouse alarm clock to ring early Tuesday morning. As the sun struggled to peek around the dark clouds, Ceebee inhaled his cat chow in the kitchenette. Noelle put on a shirtwaist dress with long sleeves and a cardigan sweater, along with gold stud earrings and a chain link choker to match, a Timex wristwatch, nude pantyhose and pumps. Where she was going, she'd look out of place in pants. On the TV her cousin had predicted rain, so Noelle slipped on a plastic raincoat that was white and decorated with large yellow stylized flowers. She let Ceebee outside to explore his domain while she gulped down a quick breakfast of coffee, orange juice and a bowl of Lucky Charms cereal with milk.

Noelle drove downtown to the three-story brick-and-stone edifice of Yuletide High School, which had educated the city's teens since the 1950s. If she hurried she might catch Mr. Baldwin, the audio-visual technician, before the school day began. He arrived early to set up equipment for the first-period classes. In her last two years of high school she had served as Mr. Baldwin's assistant, pushing the overhead and film projectors on wheeled carts to the classrooms. She'd learned how to thread eight- and sixteen-millimeter movies onto the sprocket wheels as well as how to quickly splice a broken filmstrip in a room full of belligerent students. One perk of her job was to spend her study hall period watching non-educational films on the Moviola in the A.V. office.

The tiny parking lot behind the building was reserved for teachers and staff. Most of the students walked or rode the school bus, so Noelle easily found a parking spot for the Bug only two blocks away. On her way down the sidewalk, she stopped to watch the early morning flag-raising tradition that had started before she was a student. Some customs never changed. A flagpole stood in the center of the large grassy lawn in front of the school. Teenaged boys in shirts, pants and red-and-green school letter jackets unfolded an American flag with ritual precision and hitched the cloth to the pole's rope. A little lower on the rope the boys attached a blue-and-gold Indiana state flag, and pulled the flags to the top of the pole. A white-haired gentleman stood by, his shoulders back and head held high. His piercing gray eyes observed the boys' every move. He wore an Army bomber jacket over his khaki shirt. The man shifted his weight a little, compensating with the black metal cane in his left hand.

Noelle stepped onto the grass. "Hello, Colonel." Although the man was retired from active service, the townsfolk continued to call him by his title.

Without moving, Harold Sieberson shifted his eyes to the side to identify the speaker. "'Morning, Miss McNabb."

"I see you still have the Boy Scouts on flag detail."

"Someone must instill patriotism into the kids of today." His voice was as crisp and sharp as the creases pressed into his khaki trousers. "Those young people who stage protests about our involvement in Vietnam— they're nincompoops." He laid a hand on his left thigh. "I didn't take a leg-full of Jap shrapnel in WW2 for some spoiled brats to cry like babies when asked to serve their country. America is the greatest nation in the world. We must stop the Red menace at all costs."

The flags had reached the top of the pole. A gust of wind whipped the banners straight out, and the metal clips holding the flags clunked against the pole. Noelle crossed her arms against the cool breeze. The colonel raised his right hand to his forehead to salute the flags; the boys mimicked his gesture. The veteran nudged Noelle with his elbow. She placed her right hand over her heart as she looked at the flags.

After a moment of silence, Sieberson called to the Scouts. "Dismissed!"

The boys grabbed their textbooks from where they'd left them on the ground and ran into the school building.

The army man turned his attention to Noelle. "I'm surprised to see you here, young lady. Haven't you graduated?"

"Yes, Class of '60. Colonel, I want to ask you something. You know all about the local army bases and military operations. Have you ever heard of a spy agency called SIAMESE?"

"SIAMESE?" He pushed the wire-rim glasses up his nose. "Can't say that I have. Is it one of ours?"

"Yes, I think so."

"How did you hear of it?"

What should she tell him? As a former Army officer he knew how to keep secrets, but she didn't know him well. "I met someone who said he worked for SIAMESE. It stands for Special Intelligence Apparatus for Midwest Enemy Surveillance and Espionage."

"SIAMESE? A silly name for a government organization, if you ask me. I think the man was pulling your leg."

"That's what I thought."

"Then again, it could be the code name for a special government project. With the Cold War heating up, our agencies have numerous feelers in the intelligence field. A top secret mission would not advertise its existence."

"Is there a way I can find out?"

"I keep in touch with my Army contacts. I can check into it if you wish."

"Would you please? I'd appreciate it." A sea of students surged up the concrete steps and through the open doors. "Excuse me, I have an errand to run. Maybe we can talk about this later?"

He nodded. "You know where to find me."

Sieberson made a sharp turn on the heels of his polished leather shoes and marched away. Even in retirement, the colonel still ran his life on an unwavering timetable that began each day at oh-five-hundred hours. According to the time of day, one could locate the ex-officer at a restaurant, on his daily walk, at the post headquarters of the veterans' club, inside the library among the historical stacks or at home in the evening relaxing with jazz records and a snifter of brandy.

Noelle dashed up the school steps, shoving her way past the teens. Had she look so gawky and nerdy when she was that age? She was older than those around her, but the teens were too busy talking among themselves to notice her. The endless first-floor hallway, lined with metal lockers and classroom doors, ran the length of the building. The fluorescent light tubes that hung from the high ceiling did little to brighten the otherwise dark interior. On the walls hung the posters for spirit week that would culminate in the Elves' basketball game on Friday night. The red-and-green crepe paper streamers were starting to fade. The sounds of locker doors slamming and footsteps on the linoleum floor echoed through the cavernous corridor. Noelle ran up the stairwell to reach the Audio Visual Department on the second floor. The equipment needed to run the educational records, cassette tapes, slides and films filled the too-small room. Noelle opened the wood-and-glass door and stepped inside.

The room smelled of ammonia. Mr. Baldwin was wiping the glass surface of an overhead projector with a soft rag and cleaning solution. He hadn't changed since her graduation. He was still a skinny guy in dark pants and slim tie, white long-sleeved shirt even in the summer, glasses rimmed in black plastic, dorky haircut and a constantly bemused expression. While the boilers were clanking to heat the rest of the building, the room stayed cool to preserve the filmstrips and slides. In a corner, a couple of box fans whirled a faint breeze.

"Hi, Mr. Baldwin. Remember me?"

He looked up and his face broke into a wide smile. "Well, hello, Noelle! What a surprise to see you. I thought you'd be on your way to Hollywood by now."

"I'm working on it."

"Just let me know when you're in your first movie. I'll buy a print of it for our files."

"Thanks, Mr. Baldwin."

"I've certainly missed you around here. Never had another student with your dedication. So what brings you around to the old stomping ground?"

"I need your technology." She opened her purse and pulled out the film segment. "Can you help me see what's on here?"

"Sure, no problem. What movie is it from?"

"I don't know. That's what I'm trying to find out."

Mr. Baldwin slipped on a pair of white cotton gloves before taking the celluloid strip in his fingers. "It's too short to run through the Moviola. Let's try it on the light board," a device normally used for previewing slides. He placed the strip on a slanted stand of translucent plastic and flipped a switch—the stand lit up. Mr. Baldwin picked up a magnifying glass and examined the film.

"Hard to make this out. All the frames look the same. I don't see people, just black lines that look like matchsticks. Would it be all right for me to cut off a frame and make it into a slide so we can see it better?"

"I suppose so." If the frames were identical, Hanover shouldn't fuss about losing one.

The technician laid the strip onto the film splicer and fitted it beneath the sharp cutting tool. With a finger he pushed down the cutter and neatly sliced off a single frame. He fitted the square of film into a cardboard sleeve and placed it into a slide projector. Mr. Baldwin turned on the machine, pointed the beam onto a bare spot on the wall, and focused the lens.

"I've never seen a movie still like this," he said.

The image depicted some type of machine. The device was "blown apart," with various parts separated from the main body.

"Can you make it bigger?" Noelle asked.

Mr. Baldwin pulled the cart back a couple of feet to enlarge the image. Noelle stepped closer to the wall and squinted at the picture. Words in small print filled the outer edges of the frame. Arrows ran from the words and pointed to the machine part they were meant to identify.

"This doesn't make sense," said Noelle. "I can't read these words."

Mr. Baldwin adjusted his glasses. "It's Russian. I recognize the letters as Russian, but I can't read it."

"Russian!" Maybe Hanover was right about enemy spies moving into the area. "How weird! Let's get Miss Taylor in here to read this."

"No can do. She teaches Spanish and French, but not Russian."

Noelle crossed her arms and stared at the image. "Seems odd that someone would put a picture like that on film instead of a piece of paper."

"Not necessarily. Perhaps they wanted to show it to a room full of people, like we're doing. Where did you say you found this?"

Noelle opened her mouth but closed it. She couldn't lie to her favorite teacher, but he mustn't know about Kent Calvert or SIAMESE, at least not yet. Fortunately, she was saved by the bell—the loud, clanging alarm that began and ended each class period. The principal's voice boomed over the loudspeaker in the room, welcoming the students to another school day and droning on with the morning announcements and the lunch menu. Mr. Baldwin turned a knob on the base of the wall speaker to switch off the sound.

"Afraid you'll have to go now, Noelle. I need to take the overhead down the hall for first-period American history."

A wave of emotion gripped Noelle, a memory of her own time in the ten-minute homeroom that kicked off each agonizing school day. After the announcements, the teachers took attendance and led the kids in the Pledge of Allegiance and the Lord's Prayer. During the announcements Noelle doodled in her notebook as the boys passed around dirty notes and the girls whispered just loud enough for her to overhear their catty remarks about her.

"Mr. Baldwin, is there was a way I can look at this slide later without using a projector?"

He snapped his fingers. "I have an idea."

The technician unlocked a metal cabinet and removed a bulky camera. He snapped a shot of the image on the wall. With a soft whirl the camera spit out a film pack. After waiting a few seconds for the picture to develop, Mr. Baldwin peeled off the backing on the photo. He and Noelle watched as the image magically appeared on the specially coated paper.

"Pretty nifty, isn't it? It's one of the new Polaroid Instamatic cameras. Just might eliminate the need for darkrooms. What do you think, Noelle? Is the photo readable?"

"Yeah, this is fine. Thank you."

He switched off the slide projector and tossed the photo backing into the wastebasket. "Anything for my star pupil." He placed the photo, slide and the remainder of the film clip into a white paper envelope and handed it to Noelle. She slid the packet into her handbag.

"Thanks for your help, Mr. Baldwin."

"Glad I could help. And good luck with your acting."

She bid a quick goodbye before she hurried down the stairs and through the vacant corridor. She needed to leave before the hall filled up with bleary-eyed students stumbling to their first class of the day. But as she neared the exit door, she encountered a deadly obstacle.

"Stop! Where are you going?"

Juniors and seniors with massive egos who liked to kiss up to the assistant principal were assigned as hall monitors to catch the tardies and truants. A pimply-faced boy with a "hall monitor" sash drooped across his thin chest confronted her. In one hand he held the dreaded journal where violations were recorded.

"You're supposed to be in homeroom." The monitor puffed out his chest, proud of the power he held in this position, the only time when the other kids didn't pick on him.

"Not on your life," she said. "I graduated seven years ago, so you can't give me a demerit."

"If you're a visitor, you must sign in at the office." His pubescent voice cracked. "You'll have to come to the office with me."

"I don't have time. I'm running a special errand for Mr. Baldwin." She held up the white envelope but kept it out of the boy's reach. "He needs this roll of film developed pronto or the school paper won't go to print this week." Actually, the A.V. room had its own darkroom, but she banked on the kid not knowing that.

The boy opened the journal and took a pen from the pocket protector in his shirt. "I still need your name and address."

"Minnie Mouse, Disneyland."

The first period bell rang, and Noelle shot away faster than Wile E. Coyote chasing the Roadrunner.

"Hey! Come back, you!" The monitor started after Noelle, but the flood of teens pouring out of the homerooms engulfed him and held him at bay as she left the building.

Noelle wasn't due at the record store for a while and

she didn't want to drive home and back, so she headed for The Igloo to get a bite to eat and study the photo. The structure was painted white with black lines to resembled "ice bricks." One entered the domed building through a narrow arched entryway that led to a circular room. The right side of the interior housed the drug store, with rows of shelves holding toiletries, cosmetics, small household items, greeting cards and magazines. Along the curved wall stood the pharmacy window. The soda fountain counter ran the length of the left-hand wall. In the afternoon after the schools let out, the soda shop buzzed with hungry youths eating, talking and playing hit singles on the jukebox. But for now the place was quiet and mostly empty save for the fountain stools occupied by four guys Noelle didn't want to meet.

The Brylcreem on the young men's heads made their hair so slick, a hat would have slid off. They wore faded denim jackets over their white tee-shirts. They had ripped blue jeans and soiled tennis shoes. Dirty clothes for dirty-minded people. The "bad boys" of Yuletide were still juvenile delinquents at heart. Thin wisps of smoke rose from their lit cigarettes. The quartet didn't see Noelle, as they were busy harassing the man standing behind the counter.

"Hey, Bennie, gimme a soda," said one man. "You're a good soda jerk."

"Yeah, he's a *jerk*, all right," said another man. His companions laughed. The subject of their taunt frowned and his lower lip began to quiver.

"Bennie ain't got the brains to do nothin' but jerk around with sodas," said a third guy. With his broad shoulders and thick arms, he was clearly the leader of the pack. "Ain't that right, retardo?"

Chapter 9: Strawberry Girl

Tears welled in the eyes of the man behind the counter. He carefully set down the sundae glass he was drying and wiped his hands on the pants of his white uniform. "I . . . I do a good job with the sodas. I do." He spoke emphatically but slowly, his words slightly slurred.

Noelle approached the counter. "Why don't you guys leave Bennie alone?"

The foursome swiveled on their stools to face her. "Oh, oh, oh, why don't you leave Bennie alone?" They repeated her words in a singsong voice.

"Yeah, Beanpole, why don't you leave *us* alone?" The leader used the nickname he'd given Noelle back in grade school. All through school she'd been taller than most of the boys.

"Vince, you can't even think up a good comeback line," she said.

"And who are you, Bennie's mommy?" said Vince. "Gotta stand up for Bennie 'cause he ain't got the guts to do it himself?" The guys laughed.

After Vince and his gang had dropped out of high school, the pests had continued to hang around Yuletide, supporting themselves with occasional odd jobs and seasonal farm work that required more brawn than brain. Many residents felt the troublemakers would end up behind bars, but the "bad boys," despite their tough talk, never accomplished more than petty crime.

Noelle looked at the employee. "Ignore them, Bennie. They're not half as smart as you are."

Bennie beamed with a crooked smile that revealed a couple of missing teeth. His face was freckled. His dark hair was a flyaway mess beneath the white paper cap. "Yeah? You think so?"

"I know so. Smart people don't go around insulting others."

Vince turned to his buddies. "Didda hear that? Beanpole called us stupid." He got off the stool and stomped over to Noelle. "Hey, who ya calling stupid?"

She glared at him. "Vince, why don't you and your hoods go play in the street?"

"Yeah, and *you* go play in the street, and maybe you'll get hit by a car." His tone sounded more sinister than joking.

"Is that a threat?"

A man entered from a back room. "Is there a problem here?"

Mr. Owens owned and ran The Igloo. He was also Bennie's dad and had trained him to help around the store. The lad had no education for any other job. He had repeated several grade levels. When Bennie became considerably older than the rest of the high school students, the teachers saw no reason to keep him in the classroom indefinitely and gave him a diploma out of sympathy.

"Naw, Mr. Owens, there ain't no problem at all," said Vince. "Me and my buddies, we just came in to buy some smokes."

"Then I suggest you do that and leave."

Vince snubbed out his cigarette in a glass ashtray on the counter. "Sure, we'll do that. We got lots of dough to spend."

He pulled a fat bundle of bills from his pants pocket and waved it about. Talking loudly, the quartet strolled to the pharmacy, where they each bought a pack of Marlboros.

Just as they headed for the exit door, Noelle called to them. "Hey Vince."

He turned. "Hey, what?"

"I'm still taller than you are."

He blew a raspberry at her, and the hoods left the building. Outside they revved their tricked-out motorcycles just to annoy the passers-by.

Mr. Owens said, "Is everything all right, Noelle?"

"Yeah, I'm fine. I just can't stand to watch them picking on Bennie."

"I know. He's my best employee." He put an arm around the soda jerk and hugged him. "Aren't you, Bennie?" The son smiled at his dad. "Wish there was a way to keep those punks out of my store. Last Saturday I closed up early because of the storm. Vince and his cronies were the last ones to leave. They tore out of town like maniacs. I was sure they'd crashed their bikes on the slick roads. The funny thing is, last week Vince claimed he was broke and tried to buy things on credit. I wouldn't do it, of course. But today he's flaunting a fistful of dollars. Wonder where he got it?"

Noelle frowned. If the bad boys were out during the storm, maybe they had robbed Kent. Perhaps the dead man had only given part of his cash to the robbers, and they'd shot him in retaliation.

"Mr. Owens, do you know if Vince has a gun?"

"A gun? You mean, like a hunting rifle?"

"No, a handgun."

"It's possible. When those punks were kids, they used to shoot at the birds and little animals in the woods. Not for the meat, mind you, just for meanness. But let's move on to something more cheerful. What can we do for you this morning, Noelle?"

"A strawberry shake sounds good." Her mom would scream if she knew her daughter was having dessert for breakfast.

Bennie grinned. "Yeah, okay. One strawberry milkshake coming up for my friend Noelle."

"That's a good boy, Bennie." Mr. Owens returned to the back room.

The soda jerk moved slowly and deliberately, measuring out the ingredients with care. Noelle usually tipped, so he scooped a little more ice cream than usual for her.

"Do you think it's going to rain some more, Bennie?" she asked.

"I hope not. I don't like rain. Makes me all cold and wet."

"Yeah, I like to stay dry and warm."

"Here you go." He placed a small paper circle on the counter and set the tall glass atop it. He spooned some strawberries atop the shake, and squirted on a generous dollop of whipped cream. Bennie handed her a long-handle metal spoon and a plastic straw. The shake was so thick that Noelle ate it with the spoon.

"Thanks, Bennie. You make the best milkshakes anywhere."

He smiled as she gave him a nickel tip. She walked over to the pharmacy cashier and paid fifteen cents plus sales tax for the shake. Then she carried the glass and spoon to a booth in the back where she could study the mysterious photo in private. She slid off her raincoat and hung it over the back of the booth. After Noelle ate a couple of spoonfuls of the thick, creamy delight, she pushed the glass aside and laid the photo on the table. The design looked like something she'd seen before, but couldn't place.

"And how are you today, Noelle?"

The interruption startled her. Noelle look up. Gus E. Monty stood beside the booth. One hand held a saucer with a spoon and ceramic cup on it; the other carried a brown briefcase.

She slapped both hands over the picture to hide it. "I'm fine, just fine."

"What are you looking at?"

"Nothing, nothing, just some silly picture from the family vacation last summer. You know, the twins acting stupid." She placed her purse on her lap, opened it, and pushed the photo inside. The handbag's metal closure fastened with a snap.

Gus slid into the booth, across from her. His striped suit and tie were as loud as his voice. Was he trying to imitate Elvis with that mound of black hair? "Mind if I sit here?" He picked up the glass sugar container and poured a hefty amount of sweetening into his coffee.

Noelle wanted him to scram, but he'd already settled in. "Aren't you suppose to be working today?"

"That's the beauty of selling insurance. I get out in the fresh air as much as I can. I go door to door, you know. Noelle, have you ever thought of what would happen if you suddenly died without a good life insurance policy?"

"Yeah, my cat would lose out on the fifty dollars in my savings account."

He stirred his coffee. "You're funny. But let me tell you about the beauty of insurance—you end up with more than what you pay in. Your premiums accumulate and draw interest. As I always say, a policy with Gus E. Monty is money in the bank. You can make your parents the beneficiary on the account, you know. Something to tide them over in their old age. Here, look this over." His opened his briefcase, pulled out a colorful brochure listing various insurance plans, and handed it to her.

She stuck the paper into her purse and set it on the floor. "My parents don't need my help. My dad will get a pension from the company when he retires."

"But can you count on that? Businesses have been

known to go belly up."

"Look, Gus, if you came here to rope me into buying insurance, forget it. I'm not interested."

"No, no, I just popped in to get some coffee before heading out to the new subdivision. Lots of young families are moving into town. They'll want to make sure that their kids are adequately covered just in case the worst happens."

"How thoughtful of you." She stuck a straw into her shake and took a long sip. "Say, Gus, you lived in Riverbend for a few years after high school, didn't you?"

"Sure did. That's where I learned the insurance business."

"Just by chance, did you know a guy in Riverbend named Kent Calvert?"

He starred at her with wide eyes. "Kent Calvert?"

"You act as if you know him."

"Know him? The chiseler wheedled me out of thousands of dollars."

She didn't expect that answer. "Really?"

"Did that con artist try to sell you something? If he did, I hope you told him to drop dead."

"Actually, he is dead."

"Dead?" Gus didn't sound surprised or sad.

"Murdered."

Gus dropped his friendly persona. His voice had a hard edge to it. "I can't say I'm sorry. The guy was lazy. He wanted to strike it rich with a big, one-shot scheme so he'd be set up for life. He badgered me into going into a real estate investment with him. I borrowed the money from my dad. Can't fail, Kent said. Guaranteed to triple in price. Yeah, it tripled all right. Three times zero is still zero. By the time I found out I'd been taken, Mr. Calvert was long gone. He moved away and left me busted."

"I'm sorry to hear that."

"And you know the real kicker? My boss in Riverbend heard about it and fired me. He thought I was selling bogus real estate to his clients. I was on my way up in that company. I was on the fast track to becoming regional manager. But after that fiasco, the only place I could get a job was back in this two-bit town. So much for the big city lights. And my dad is still bugging me about repaying the money."

"You're not doing all that badly in Yuletide, are you? Not with all those young families moving in."

"That's true." Gus downed the last of his coffee, made a loud smacking noise of pleasure, grabbed a handful of napkins from the silver metal holder on the table, and wiped his mouth. "Gotta run." His perky salesman persona popped back into place. "Need to hit up at least three blocks before lunch."

"By the way, Gus, didn't you tell me you were out driving Saturday night? On your way back from Indy?"

"Yeah, so what?"

"I heard there was a shooting on Ornament Lane that night. Did you happen to see it?"

"No. I was on the other side of town. That's the first I've heard of any shooting. Anyway, I gotta run. My clients await."

Gus departed, leaving his dishes on the table for Bennie to bus later. Noelle nibbled on a spoonful of the shake. Some time ago Gus had mentioned in passing that he owned a gun because sometimes he carried large sums of money in his work. Maybe as Gus was driving home he'd found Kent Calvert walking along the road and—. But as much as Noelle disliked the man, she couldn't picture him as a killer. After all, he was a member of her church. Then again, it seemed the only reason he showed up on Sundays was to hawk his wares to the other parishioners. Gus had a dark side she hadn't seen before.

Chapter 10: Incense and Peppermints

Business at the record store was slow, but steady enough to keep Noelle's mind off Kent Calvert. She also picked up a bit of news for her bratty sister: a new Monkees album would be on the shelves in a few months. Noelle shuddered. Last year at the release of *More of the Monkees*, every pre-teen girl in town was at the counter, screaming for a copy of the sold-out disc. Maybe Noelle could take a vacation on the release date of this new piece of noise.

At five o'clock Noelle clocked out for the day and drove to the hippies' farm. She took Ornament Lane but kept on driving past her driveway. She went by the giant Kris Kringle statue and the sign that read WELCOME TO YULETIDE, SANTA'S YEAR-ROUND HOME. The hippies deliberately settled on land just outside the city limits to keep Chief Whitlock off their backs. She turned onto an unpaved road, thickly lined with trees, that led to a two-story farmhouse with a garden and fruit trees behind it. She parked the Bug beside the vehicle the hippies used for transportation: an old hearse retired from a local funeral home. They had repainted the vehicle with swirls of color on the outside, and hung beads and crystals from the rearview mirror inside. From behind the house came the sounds of bleating goats, clucking chickens and a barking dog. The front door was unlocked, as usual, so Noelle strolled in without knocking. Nobody inside would have heard her knock anyway, due to the acid rock blaring from a cassette tape recorder inside the kitchen. A young woman in an East Indian caftan stood over the gas stove, stirring a pan full of thick stew. A hand-woven headband kept her long blond hair out of her eyes.

The woman shouted over the music. "Noelle! Hey babe, what's happening?"

"Hi, Moonbaby. Did Rambler tell you that he invited me over for supper?"

"No, but that's not a surprise. The lunk can barely remember to put on his pants in the morning."

"If I'm imposing—"

"No way, come on in! We've always got plenty of grub. Take a seat."

Noelle eased onto one of the rickety wooden stools, fearful it might collapse. She kept her coat on, as the room was a bit cool. The only heat in the house came from the kitchen stove, a wood-burning stove in the bedroom and a fireplace in the living room. Today, only the kitchen stove was in use. Smoke rose from the square metal incense burner that held a burning cone of patchouli. Moonbaby turned down the volume on the tape player. She poured a glass of strangely colored liquid from a glass pitcher.

Noelle accepted the offered drink and sniffed the mixture cautiously. "What is it?"

"Carrot and beet juice. Made fresh today."

She sipped before taking a bigger swallow. The hippies were generous hosts, but their tastes were more exotic than Mrs. McNabb's traditional home cooking.

Noelle nodded at the tape player. "I recognize that. It's the new Grateful Dead album. We played it once at the record store. Chief Whitlock threatened to close us down if we did it again."

Moonbaby shook her head. "The pigs are so uptight."

"Where's Rambler?"

"He's out fixing the water pump. The well water's a little murky."

Rambler strolled in through the back door, his blue jeans and denim shirt soaked with dirty water. The ever-present bandana tied around his head was drenched with sweat. He set a wrench and a metal pail in a corner.

He wiped his forearm across his forehead. "That was a chore. Thought I'd have to climb down in the well to patch it up. Hey, Noelle. Nice to see ya." He smiled, revealing a mouthful of teeth that hadn't seen a dentist in years.

"Hi, Rambler. Did you get the pump fixed?"

"Hope so. Either that or we gotta buy water from The Man. That's a drag." He leaned over the pan and sniffed. "Hey, woman, that smells good. What is it?"

"Millet casserole," replied Moonbaby. "You go and get cleaned up. You're not eating in those grubby clothes. We got company present. Now scoot!"

She affectionately swatted his rump. He, in turn, grabbed her around the waist and pulled her in for a smooch. Then he stomped up the stairs, muttering.

"Don't mind him." Moonbaby turned off the tape player. "I think the stork dropped him on his head when he was a kid."

Noelle laughed. She helped Moonbaby carry the mismatched ceramic plates and mugs and wooden cutlery to the glassed-in porch and set three places around the wooden picnic table. Noelle liked the porch, which had a terrific view of the garden and surrounding woods. Moonbaby brought out the casserole as well as a plate with slabs of homemade whole grain bread and a bowl of apple butter.

By the time the women finished setting the table, Rambler returned, clad in pants from a surplus Army store, a stripped shirt and sandals. Moonbaby brought out three glasses of the vegetable juice. Noelle sat on one side of the table and the couple on the other. After the three filled their plates and began eating, Noelle asked about Kent Calvert.

Rambler started the story. "Saturday we hit Riverbend to stock up on stuff at the health food store. We wuz driving home in the sloppy rain. It's dark and nasty out. I sees this kid on the side of the road, drenched to the bone. I figure, what kind of fool's out in this weather? I figure something's up. I sees a duffle bag in his hand and figure he's on the lam from the fuzz. I can dig it, so I pull over to pick up the dude."

Moonbaby interrupted. "We pick up hitchhikers all the time. They're good company."

"Hey, woman, I'm the one telling this story!"

"So tell it right."

He rambled on. "The kid's bummed at the idea of riding in a hearse, but there's this big thunder boom, see, so he hops right in. He's dripping water on the back seat and getting mud on the floor. Every time a cop car passes, kid ducks behind the seat."

Moonbaby said, "I tried talking to the kid—"

"Hey, close yer trap!"

"Why don't you have seconds and shut up?"

"Watch it, woman! Any more sass outta of you, I'm ditchin' you by the side of the road!"

"Promises, promises."

Rambler spooned another helping of casserole onto his plate and ate as Moonbaby picked up the tale.

"I tried talking to the kid, but he clammed up. Wouldn't give us his name at first. We brought him here. He didn't want to come in, but I said we wouldn't let him go another mile until he dried out and filled his belly. Poor kid was shaking with cold, and he looked like he hadn't eaten in days. I heated up some vegetable soup and fixed some peanut butter and honey sandwiches—"

"I made the sandwiches," said Rambler.

"So you did. I poured some hot cocoa in the kid to warm him up. Ramble built a fire, and the kid sat in the beanbag chair by the fireplace to thaw out."

Rambler spoke. "Once the cat gets fed, he starts rapping. Says his name's Kent Calvert and he's truckin' to Indy 'cause he's got somethin' he's gotta give to someone. I says, 'How come you ditched the bus?' He says the cops are after him for something he did and stakin' out the bus station. I says, 'Dude, you must have ripped off something righteous if the fuzz are on your tail.'"

Noelle asked, "Did he say what he had that he had to turn over?"

"You mean like contraband?" Rambler shook his head. "No way, man. This dude was so clean he squeaked when he walked. We offered him some Mary Jane to help him relax. He turned us down flat."

"I don't mean he was smuggling dope," said Noelle. "Maybe he had something else."

Moonbaby buttered a slice of bread. "Like what?"

From the blank looks on their faces, Noelle could tell they had no idea what she meant. If Kent had the film clip, he didn't tell them. "Never mind."

Moonbaby swallowed a bite of bread and continued. "After a while Kent said he had to split. We told him he could sleep in the basement. But he wanted to push on."

Rambler cut in. "Said if he thumbed rides in the dark, the cops wouldn't see him. So the kid takes his duffle and shuffles out the door." He looked at his partner. "We got any dessert?"

Moonbaby retreated to the kitchen and returned with a spoon and a pan of fresh-out-of-the-oven blueberry cobbler. Noelle scooped out a huge helping of the tasty dessert for herself.

"That poor man," said Moonbaby. "I had a premonition something awful was going to happen to him. I warned him not to leave, but he wouldn't listen."

Noelle said, "Did someone give him a ride from your house?"

"Nope," said Rambler. "Least ways not that we saw. You can't see the road from the house. If some dude picked him, we missed it."

Moonbaby pushed the pan of cobbler close to Noelle. "Here, have seconds."

"Thanks, but I'm stuffed," she said. "You need to tell Chief Whitlock what you know about Kent."

Rambler's eyes bugged out. "Are you crazy, man? No way! He'd say we wuz the ones that bumped off the kid. That pig's lookin' for any excuse to lock us up."

"No one can testify that they saw you shoot Kent," said Noelle.

"Nobody can say we didn't."

"That's right, Noelle," said Moonbaby. "The cops don't believe anything we say. Besides, we never saw who killed the kid. What can we say?"

"Whoever shot Kent did it between your house and mine. And that was at, what time?" The hippies looked at each other. "Do you even have a clock in the house?"

"He left about seven-twenty-five," said Moonbaby. "The kid looked at his watch when he left."

"Great," said Noelle, with little confidence. "All we have to do is find out who was driving down Ornament Lane late Saturday night in bad weather." She consulted her wristwatch. "And speaking of driving down Ornament Lane, I need to get home and feed my cat. Thanks for supper. It was delicious."

"Anytime," said Moonbaby. "Don't bother cleaning up. We'll manage."

Rambler laughed. "Yeah, we'll just add this to the stack of dirty dishes already piled up in the sink."

Back at the cottage, Noelle changed out of her nice clothes and into blue jeans with rolled-up cuffs and a dark blue college sweatshirt. She fed the ravenous Ceebee and, sitting at the kitchenette table, glanced through the mail and the daily newspaper. Nothing exciting in the letters, and the paper still had no word about Kent's murder. How could the paper miss someone's death? SIAMESE must be keeping the incident out of the media. When the fat cat had finished sucking in his food, he sat by Noelle's feet and cleaned up. She studied the picture made from Kent's film clip. The sketch resembled the assembly drawings she'd seen in the technical journals her dad brought home from the plant, but she couldn't identify the type of machine. She went outside to clear her head.

In the yard she sat in an old metal glider, rocking gently. Out in the country, the squeaking sounds of the rusty glider didn't bother any neighbors. Ceebee jumped in her lap; she absently petted him. Away from the glare of city lights, the stars sparkled in the clear night sky; the moon shone clearly. Chirping crickets and ha-rummping frogs made a pleasant sound. As a kid she would lie on a blanket in her parents' backyard and make up stories about the man in the moon. Too bad the moon guy couldn't tell her who killed Kent. The moon may have been the only witness to the murder. A blinking light overhead caught her eye. The light quickly moved across the sky. Was it the Russian Sputnik or the Telstar? All these satellites overhead watching on her. And then Kent's picture made sense.

The photo made from the filmstrip was a diagram of a spy satellite.

Chapter 11: Ask Me Why

Noelle dumped Ceebee onto the ground and dashed into the house faster than a shopper glomming onto an in-store hourly discount. She picked up a library book; she'd used a certain business card for a bookmark. Noelle dialed the number on the card.

A woman with a Kentucky accent spoke in a monotone. "State your name, please."

"If I said Tabby Gray was calling for Fido Brown, would you know what I was talking about?"

The voice remained calm and unruffled. Noelle surmised the operator had received every type of bizarre call possible. "Yes, ma'am. What is your message?"

"Tell Fido to get over here pronto. We need to talk."

"I'll relay the message." The line went dead. If anyone was listening in, they didn't have time to trace the call.

Noelle realized she hadn't told the operator where "here" was, but Hanover probably knew already. The satellite that had just passed overhead had probably taken her photo and relayed it to SIAMESE headquarters. Noelle wasn't sure if Hanover would really show up, so she went about her business. She slipped The Beatles' *Help* LP from its paper sleeve and put it on the turntable. She owned a nice hi-fi system with twin speakers, nothing like her sister's cheap portable. While the music played, she practiced some tricks with Ceebee. By the time the needle neared the inner groove, someone knocked on the door. The tone arm returned automatically and the machine shut off as Noelle opened the door. Without an invitation or a greeting, Hanover rushed in. This time his suit was navy. He needed to expand his wardrobe.

"What did you want to tell me?" he said.

His abrupt manner annoyed her. In spite of Hanover's gun, he no longer frightened her.

"I'm fine, how are you?" Hopefully he'd pick up the sarcasm in her voice. Noelle sat down on the sofa. Ceebee didn't hide, but snuggled beside his servant and kept his yellow eyes locked on the stranger.

"In my work, I don't have time for niceties. You have something to tell me?"

"I have something to *show* you." She picked up the white envelope from the coffee table and pulled out the filmstrip, carefully handling it by the edges, and held it up for him to see. "Is this what you're looking for?"

He took the celluloid from her hands and held it to the floor lamp for inspection. "Where did you find this?" He didn't sound happy, excited, disappointed or any other emotion.

"Under my sofa. When Kent was here, my cat must have taken the film out of his pocket and hidden it. That picture on the film is a spy satellite, isn't it?"

"Miss McNabb, I'm afraid you know too much."

Her stomach tightened. "Does that mean you're going to kill me?"

For the first time since they'd met, he gave a hint of a smile. "No. Of course not. At SIAMESE we never harm civilians unless they are working against us. But the more you know, the more vulnerable you become to our enemies."

"Does that mean a spy is going to kill me?"

"Not if we can help it." He snatched the envelope from her, placed the film clip inside, and slipped it into his inner jacket pocket. Noelle wanted to keep the photo and slide to study later, but she felt Hanover would flip his lid if she did.

"So what's on the other missing microdots?" she said. "More satellite plans?"

"I can't say. Thank you for your help, Miss McNabb. I appreciate that you called me as soon you recovered the strip. Goodbye."

She jumped to her feet. "That's it? That's all you're going to say? What about Kent Calvert's death?"

"What about it?"

"Do you have any leads on who killed him?"

"At this moment our priority is to locate the rest of the missing data. The young man's killer is not as critical."

"A man is murdered and you don't care?"

"Kent Calvert is dead. Identifying his assailant will not change that fact, whether we find the killer tomorrow or ten years from now."

"What about Kent's family? They want to know. They need closure."

"Miss McNabb, in my work I frequently deal with death. A number of agents I knew personally have been eliminated in the line of duty. We accept it and move on. Meeting our mission goals is more important and productive that wallowing in grief."

"You're a cold fish."

"And you're a passionate young lady. I respect that."

"Have *you* killed anyone?"

He didn't reply, but the hard look in his eyes answered the question—and frightened her.

She sat down quickly, almost squashing the cat. "Anyway, that filmstrip proves that a spy did not kill Kent Calvert."

"Why do you say that?"

"A spy would have taken the film out of his pocket."

"Not necessarily. The enemy may not have searched

hard enough."

"My cat found it right away."

Hanover took a seat on the recliner. "The boy might have escaped after he was shot."

"A kid with a bullet in his chest is not going to outrun the scum who shot him. Maybe the killer wanted Kent dead for another reason besides the film."

"Why does this matter to you?"

Noelle paused. "I'm not sure. I guess when someone almost dies in my house, I feel responsible."

"Acting as a Good Samaritan is not always a noble thing. You may be the next one in need of assistance."

"You've been a spy for too long. You see the bad side of everyone."

"I call it healthy suspicion. The first rule I learned as an agent was that people are not always what they seem to be. My theory is that Kent Calvert is dead because he trusted the wrong person. But what I think is not important. What matters is that we find the missing information quickly. Since you seem anxious to help, perhaps we can use you."

"Me? What can I do?"

Hanover shifted in the chair. "Normally we don't involve civilians, but you already know a great deal, and I can trust you."

"I thought you were suspicious of everyone."

"At first, yes. But after our initial investigation, your character checked out positive." She opened her mouth to ask about the 'investigating' part—when had he been checking up on her? He kept talking. "We need to move fast, but we're short on manpower. Due to an unusually high number of assignments, we only have two available female agents. One broke her leg recently and is out of the field."

"You want me to be a spy? I mean, an agent? But I know nothing about the spy business."

"It's a simple undercover job. A seasoned agent will be with you. She will do the work. Your role will be to act as backup."

"If you have her, why do you need me?"

"Agents always work in pairs. If one is injured or captured or his cover's blown, the other can give aid or take over the mission. A civilian can also add credibility to the cover."

"I couldn't do that. Work undercover, I mean."

"Of course you can. You're an actress. You'll be portraying a character for a live audience. Think of this as the most important role you've ever played."

The offer piqued her interest. An acting role? Something more challenging that playing the Winter Witch for a bunch of bored, tired kids? If Noelle could pass herself off as another person in a real-life setting, she'd have something to crow about. She would indeed be a great actress.

She straightened her posture. "What do I need to do?"

"An enemy agent by the code name Bulldog has offered to sell information to us."

"A double cross."

"So to speak. He knows the location of one of the microdots. But we have to move carefully. If we tip our hand, the enemy may intercept Bulldog before he has a chance to talk to us."

"Sounds dangerous."

"Not if you're careful. As an actress you know how to stay focused in the moment and be attentive to the other actors. That's what you'd be doing. Bulldog is willing to meet us at a nightclub in Riverbend. Tomorrow night you and the other agent will go there, posing as go-go dancers. Your partner will make contact with Bulldog and find out what he knows. If his information is legitimate, your work is finished."

A go-go dancer? In high school she used to attend the Saturday night sock hops at The Barn, an old wooden farm building on the outskirts of town that had been converted into a dance hall. She enjoyed listening to the local bands play cover versions of the current hits, but seldom had the chance to dance. The guys never asked her for a dance except on the slow numbers just so they could grope and squeeze her.

"Tomorrow night? What about my job at the record store? If I'm out dancing all night, I'll be too bushed for Thursday morning."

"I'll inform your supervisor that you've accepted a temporary acting role in Riverbend. I'll make sure that you retain your job. SIAMESE will, of course, compensate you financially for any work done in our behalf."

"Mom will flip out when she hears I'm working as a spy."

"She must not know. You cannot tell anyone about your work with us. Ever. That's an absolute requirement and is not negotiable."

"Why can't I tell my friends? I might get some respect."

Hanover's frown deepened. "No. Like a cat, SIAMESE works in stealth and solitude. If our involvement is made public, we are no longer effective."

"But I tell my mom everything. If she asks what I'm doing tomorrow night, what do I say to her?"

"Tell her anything except what you're really doing."

"You mean lie?"

"Withhold the truth."

"You don't have any morals, do you?"

"If I had no ethics, I'd be with the CIA. Miss McNabb, you lie every day in your acting job. When you're on stage you ask the audience to believe that you are someone other than your real self. Everyone in this town lies by saying Santa Claus is real and lives at the theme park."

"That's only make believe. It's harmless fun. Acting isn't the same as these spy games."

"Be that as it may, if you can't keep our work confidential, you are of no use to us."

Noelle wasn't happy about working with a group that was more secretive than the Masons, but staying close to Hanover might help her find out what had happened to Kent Calvert.

"How do I know you're not really working for the other side? How can I trust *you*?"

"We're very much alike, Miss McNabb. We have a common heritage. I have no time to explain that now. Will you work with us, and can I rely on your discretion?"

"Yes, I'm in."

"Good girl. I have one more question for you."

"What's that?"

"Can you dance?"

Chapter 12: Magical Mystery Tour
Wednesday

Before Hanover left, he said he'd pick up Noelle the next morning for a briefing at SIAMESE headquarters. She tried to get a good night's sleep, but was too excited and nervous about her undercover job. Would her job be as exhilarating as the spy shows she'd watched on TV? Would the bad guys capture her? Who was this partner she'd be working with—someone male and cute?

Early Wednesday morning she paid a visit to her landlords' house. The couple had returned from their trip, and they agreed to feed Ceebee while she was away that night. They often took care of the cat whenever Noelle was off on family vacations. She couldn't leave a bowl of cat food outside for Ceebee because the neighborhood possums, raccoons, mice and squirrels would gobble it first. Back at the cottage, Noelle thought about what a spy should wear to work. Should she dress like Emma Peel of *The Avengers* or Agent 99 of *Get Smart*? She settled for a belted dress with cap sleeves and pencil skirt along with a matching sweater decorated with floral embroidery. She tried on a wool felt wide brim hat; she could pull the brim over her eyes to hide her face from the enemy. She put on her rings, a watch, gold earrings and a delicate neck chain with a gold initial "N." Makeup included foundation, rouge and red lipstick. Go-go dancers were glamorous, so she carefully glued on a set of long fake eyelashes. Just as she finished setting her face with a puff of face powder came the crunch of car tires on the gravel driveway. Why didn't she hear the car engine? Noelle pulled on a gray raincoat to protect against the drizzle outside, grabbed her purse, opened the door— and found Hanover standing there already.

"Hello. I was just on my way out," she said.

"I need to come inside."

"Why?"

Hanover pushed past her and headed straight for the Princess phone. He picked up the receiver and placed a round metal disk on the mouthpiece.

Noelle put her hands on her hips. "What are you doing to my phone?"

Hanover ignored her and followed the phone line to the wall jack. He unplugged the line, stuck a small metal cube in the jack, and inserted the end of the line into the device.

"I'm securing your phone," he said. "We need a safe way to communicate. Calls on open lines can be tapped, traced and recorded. Do not remove the devices from your phone. Understood?"

"Are these gizmos going to interfere with my normal calls?"

"Absolutely not. The caller on the other end will hear no difference. When you place a call, just dial the number as you usually do."

"What about the other people on the party line? They'll be snooping like they always do."

"The devices will move all your calls onto a private line. You can phone at any time without waiting for another person to hang up."

"Hey, that's great. Those old ladies can jabber for hours. But does that mean you'll be listening to my regular calls?"

"No need to do so. Your conversations are not that interesting or vital to our national interests."

"So you've been nosing in on my calls!"

"Not just you, Miss McNabb. We periodically scan other local calls as well. Don't worry. We did not record your calls. As I said, the talk was of no importance to us."

"Thanks, I think." Noelle crossed her arms, wondering if she wanted to go through with this caper. "My life must be too boring for you spy guys."

He ignored the jab. "Do not contact SIAMESE from an unsecured line. Only call us from this phone."

Hanover rushed out the door. Noelle shrugged. He must not be married—no wife would tolerate his odd behavior. She locked the door behind her and stepped over Ceebee, who had jumped on the porch as Hanover headed for the car. Noelle bent over to scratch the cat on his head and reminded him to be a good boy. He merely stretched his front paws, yawned, and sprawled out to catch some sun on the porch.

The black sedan idled silently in the drive. No wonder Hanover could slip in and out of places unseen—and unheard. Hanover, dressed in a crisp white shirt, burgundy suit and tie, and black raincoat, held open the back door of the sedan and motioned for her to get in. After she slid in, he sat beside her and closed the door.

"If you're back here, who's driving?" she asked.

"Another agent."

She looked for the driver, but a black Plexiglas barrier on the back of the front seat blocked her view. She turned her head. The backseat and rear windows were likewise darkened.

"Hey! I can't see out!"

"For your protection. So you can't be seen with me, and to hide the location of SIAMESE headquarters. The less you know, the less you can reveal to the enemy."

"I thought you said this job wasn't dangerous."

"Everything about life has its risks. What if you tripped on stage during your show at the park and broke your leg?"

Noelle eyed him. "How did you know—have you seen the show?"

"Of course. Our background check on you was quite thorough."

"I never saw you in the audience."

"You were not supposed to see me."

She was about to ask him how he liked her acting when the car moved. "Why can't I hear the engine?"

"We modified the motor so we can run surveillance and pickups in silence."

She jiggled the door handle. A wave of panic hit. "You locked me in so I can't escape!"

"The doors are bolted to prevent the enemy from entering the car from the outside. We are not kidnapping you. If you wish to abort the mission at any time prior to reaching headquarters, just say so. The driver will pull over, and you will be free to go. However, once you leave the car, you will sever all ties with SIAMESE. We will have no further contact with you."

And no opportunity to find out who killed Kent Calvert. Noelle leaned back in the cushy black leather seat and tried to determine their location by the movement of the car, but the endless turns and loops made her dizzy. No doubt the driver was taking a roundabout route just to confuse her.

"I can't hear the traffic outside," she said.

"The car is soundproofed to keep our talk confidential."

"Am I really going to see your headquarters, or just a little rented room you're pretending is your office?"

Her tone didn't faze him. "Obviously you won't see the entire complex. The laboratories, files, computers and weapons rooms are off limited to non-classified personnel."

"You guys can keep a secret better than my parents when they buy Christmas presents. I bet Dash Hanover isn't your real name."

"You're right."

"Aha! Even your name is phony."

"Only for practical reasons. My surname is fictitious to prevent the enemy from tracing my family and possibly harming them."

"Your real name can't be Dash. What parent would give their kid a goofy name like Dash?"

A flicker of annoyance crossed his face as he turned to face her. "Why are you so inquisitive?"

"You know everything about me. It's only fair I should know a little about you."

"What you know at present is sufficient. Besides, we've arrived at our destination. No more time for talk." How Hanover could determine their location without seeing through the windows was a mystery. The sedan stopped. "And I recommend you close your eyes."

"Come on, there's no need for that. If you don't trust me, just blindfold me. I can't see through these tinted windows and—aaaggghhh!"

An intense light probed the car's interior. Hanover placed his palms on his knees, shut his eyes and patiently waited. Noelle tried to shield her eyes with her hands, but too late. The light was blinding.

"I warned you," he said.

"Holy cow! What was that?"

The light faded. "You may open your eyes now. It's a security precaution. If an enemy agent had stolen this vehicle or was holding us hostage, the scan would detect the unauthorized person inside and the vehicle would not be permitted to enter the facility."

Noelle rubbed her eyes. She blinked several times as bright dots danced in front of her eyeballs. The car lurched forward and took a nosedive down a ramp. Noelle grabbed the front edge of the seat as she flattened against the back of the seat. With a thud the car hit a subterranean floor, bounced, drove a few yards and stopped. After a moment, both of the passenger side doors swung open automatically. Noelle glanced at Hanover. He nodded. She gingerly stepped out; the car door closed behind her.

Hanover walked around the vehicle and stood beside her. "Welcome to SIAMESE headquarters."

She expected to see rows of computers or tables full of gadgets and lab equipment, but only saw cars. "Looks like a parking garage."

"It is. Come this way."

Deep underground, the rain didn't affect them. Noelle unbuttoned her raincoat and let it hang loose. Their footsteps echoed between the gray steel walls. They passed rows of black sedans, coupes, convertibles, flatbed trucks and family sedans for use in undercover assignments.

"With all of these cars, you must have a lot of people around," she said. "Why do you need me?"

"Most of our employees work internally. Each field agent requires a vast support network of experts in communications, weapons, transportation, research, linguistics, cryptography and other areas. Besides, very few applicants pass the training program for field work."

"Then what makes you think I can do this?"

"Because you're highly intelligent. We can mold you."

She opened her mouth to respond. *Mold me into a killing machine like James Bond?* But she said nothing because they had reached a door. Hanover pressed his hands on a ledge and a light scanned his palm and fingerprints. He stared into a beam that checked his retina to complete the identification process. After pressing a passcode onto a keypad in the wall, a door slid open with a whoosh. They stepped inside an entryway. As the door closed behind them, Hanover opened a closet to their left. They hung up their raincoats. On the right-hand wall, rows of hooks held black lanyards with rectangular badges. Hanover placed the one purple-colored badge around his neck and handed a yellow visitor's badge to Noelle.

"Keep this around your neck at all times," he said.

She slid the badge over her head. "It's kinda bulky. Why do I need this? You know who I am."

"Yes, but our internal security system does not. The badge sends out a continuous radio signal. If our monitors pick up the thermal heat pattern of a life form with no signal, lasers will attack the foreign body."

"Oh dear." Just being inside SIAMESE headquarters was deadly.

The door in front of them slid opened to admit them into the facility itself. Noelle clutched the badge tightly against her chest. She glanced at the bare walls, searching for the laser guns. Rows of fluorescent tubes in the ceiling illuminated a seemingly endless hall of gray walls and floor. A few people passed by, all wearing badges of various colors. Some greeted Hanover, and he nodded in return. Some held clipboards; others carried boxes or weapons, and all seemed intent on reaching their destination quickly. Another door opened. They entered a sparse conference room comprised of bare white walls and gray carpeting. Swivel chairs made of chrome tubing surrounded a metal conference table.

"I hope this job isn't as drab as this building," said Noelle. "Don't you have any color around here?"

The hall door opened again to reveal a tall, black woman, as lithe—and as dangerous—as a panther. An orange bell-bottom jumpsuit, cinched with a black patent leather belt, clung to her long, lean body. A red field agent badge hung around her neck. Gold hoops decorated her earlobes. A metal pick was stuck in the back of her trimmed Afro. Her flats made no sound as she strode across the carpeting. Noelle felt an energy radiating from the woman, who seemed coiled up and ready to spring into action. The piercing black eyes scared her.

Hanover said, "Noelle, meet your partner, Destiny King."

The black woman ran her eyes up and down Noelle. Her lips tightened. Was she angry, disappointed or confused? Noelle couldn't read the woman's expression.

Destiny held out a palm. "Noelle, slip me some skin!" She said this as a command, not an invitation.

Noelle gently slapped the offered palm and turned over her own hand. Destiny returned the greeting with a strong smack on her palm.

"Ladies, let's get seated and start the briefing," Hanover said.

He took a chair at one end of the table. Destiny slid into a chair along the side, and Noelle sat beside her partner. A panel slid open in the wall facing them, revealing a huge TV monitor. Destiny removed the pick and laid it on the table.

"That's a beautiful pick." Noelle reached for it.

"Don't touch that!" Destiny snatched the pick from her.

"I'm sorry. I didn't think you'd mind."

"When you're working with SIAMESE, you gotta be careful. A girl could get hurt." The agent pressed one of the colored stones on the handle of the silver pick. Thin razor blades shot out from between the tines. Noelle leaned back in her chair and gasped.

"Dash should have warned you." Destiny shot the operative a glance. "Most everything we wear or carry is a weapon or communication device."

Noelle said, "Mr. Hanover, am I going to get some nifty gadgets like that?"

"No," he said. "Agents first must be trained in the use of our specialized equipment. In the hands of amateurs, these devices could backfire."

Noelle frowned. "I'll be careful."

"Besides, you won't need weapons. This mission is pretty straight forward with minimal jeopardy."

Hanover pushed a button on the table. The room lights dimmed. A slide appeared on the monitor. "This is your target. The Funky Feline, a nightclub in downtown Riverbend."

The slide showed a door with peeling red paint and faded drawings of cats dancing on their back paws.

"It looks seedy," said Noelle.

"It is." Hanover clicked a button and a second slide showed the club interior, a smoky room jammed with small round tables encircled by low stools. On each side of a small bandstand rose a column topped with a tall gilt cage.

"Each of you will be dancing in one of these cages." Hanover glanced at Noelle. "Have you any problems with claustrophobia?"

She considered the cramped dressing rooms and tiny stages she'd endured while performing in various theatrical productions. She replied no, and the operative continued.

"After we finish this briefing, you'll have a run-through of various dance steps so your performance will look professional. You'll work a forty-five minute shift followed by a ten-minute break. During the break,

Miss King will contact this man."

The slide changed. The monitor didn't seem big enough to hold the enormous man. His fat jowls hung like bags of sand, and his sagging eyelids almost hid his squinty eyes.

"Bulldog will be seated at one of the tables," said Hanover.

"What do I say to him?" Not that Noelle wanted to deal with such an unappealing slob.

"I'll do the rapping," said Destiny. "You just hang back and watch out for trouble."

The room lights turned on and the panel slid back over the monitor. Hanover continued. "Once Bulldog hands off the information, there's no need for you girls to continue dancing. Get out of there as quickly as you can. Destiny will take Noelle home, then report back here."

Noelle was incredulous. "That's it? Just dance? That's all you want me to do?"

"That's all," he said.

"That isn't much."

Destiny said, "Sometimes the easiest missions are the hardest."

Hanover dismissed the women. They headed down the hallway to the gym for the dance lesson. When they finished, Destiny offered to take Noelle home and pick her up later for the assignment.

Noelle checked her Timex. "Is that the time? Didn't know it was so late. Don't take me home. I have someplace to go before we head for Riverbend."

"Where's that?"

"It's Wednesday night. I'm going to church."

Chapter 13: Everybody's Talkin'

In an effort to appeal to the younger generation, the Old Beth council had recently revised the traditional Wednesday night service into something more informal and interactive. At six o'clock, everyone gathered in the fellowship hall—a huge open room in the basement used for dinners, wedding receptions and the Boy and Girl Scout troops—for a potluck dinner and singing. The participants then split for age-appropriate programs in different rooms. The kids played games and made crafts. The teens held a rap session and listened to records of contemporary Jesus music. The adults had three options: choir practice, the Marriage and Family Class or the Modern Social Issues discussion group that was supposed to reflect on world affairs, but after ten minutes usually drifted into local gossip.

The black sedan slid unseen and unheard into an alley behind the church. During the trip from SIAMESE headquarters, Hanover once again rode in the back seat along with Noelle. He answered her questions about the assignment but shared nothing about himself. The less she knew about him, the more she was intrigued. Was he really just a calculating machine, or did a human heart beat beneath that bulletproof vest? Tonight she'd ask Destiny to tell her more about the mystery man. If he wasn't so uptight, she might even go for him. He was cute.

Noelle left the car and entered the church through a back door. A short flight of steps led into the fellowship hall. She'd arrived late, but that only meant everyone else had hit the buffet first; she wouldn't have to wait in line. The din of many conversations filled the room. Framed reproductions of Warner Sallman's paintings of Christ hung on the wood-paneled walls. After dodging the tykes running about, Noelle grabbed a paper plate at one end of a long table loaded with pans of homemade casseroles, pot roasts, chicken and dumplings, garden salads, fruit Jell-O and rolls. A separate table nearly sagged under the weight of pies, brownies, cookies and fudge. Her parents had saved her a seat at one of the folding tables set up in the center of the room. Noelle greeted her parents, sat down and dug into her food. At SIAMESE headquarters she hadn't had a chance to eat lunch, and she needed energy for the busy night ahead.

"So how was your day at the store?" Mom asked.

Noelle stopped chewing her food and tried to remember the alibi that Hanover had concocted for her. "Ummm, I had an acting job in Riverbend."

"That's nice! Is it a play or—"

"It's a TV commercial. Might keep me busy for the rest of the week."

Mom salted the green bean casserole on her plate. "A whole week to shoot a commercial?"

"Well, you know, there's a lot of reshoots and stuff. Where are the twins?" Noelle had to change the subject. The more she lied to her mom, the worse she felt. Eventually she'd have to break down and tell the truth.

"They're sitting with the other kids." Dad used his fork to point to a noisy table in the corner. "What's the commercial about?"

"Something about cars."

For the first time ever, Noelle was relieved when Gus E. Monty slid into the empty chair beside her. At least he wouldn't be quizzing her about top-secret matters.

"Hi! Is this seat taken?" Gus grinned like a circus

clown; apparently he'd had a successful day selling insurance to the new homeowners.

"It is now," Noelle replied.

"I'm surprised to see you here. I didn't spot your car in the parking lot."

Drat! She hadn't thought of that. Her VW was so unique that everyone in town recognized it. "The Bug's in the shop. I hitched a ride with a friend."

"Really? Your car was running fine yesterday."

"You know how cars are, temperamental and all."

Gus squinted at her. "And you keep telling me lies."

Noelle stared back. How could he know about SIAMESE? "I don't know what you're talking about."

"You told me you were busy on Wednesday nights, but here you are."

She breathed a sigh of relief. "What I meant to say was, I'm not free for dates on Wednesdays."

"We can still go out for a cup of coffee when this is over."

"I'm busy."

"Doing what?"

That caught her short. Gus knew that after church both the park and the record store would be closed. "I have to go home and write letters and stuff."

"You can write letters any time. Say, I dropped by the record store today and didn't see you."

Why was everyone suddenly interested in her workday? "I saw you coming and escaped through a trap door in the floor. Now if you'll excuse me, I need to get some dessert."

Noelle hadn't finished her meal and wasn't ready for sweets, but she had to get away from the interrogation. She headed for the dessert table and slowly mused over the offerings. Then the Old Beth band of high school students began to play. Noelle drifted back to the table without taking any goodies, relieved that she wouldn't have to carry on a conversation over the loud music.

The group had three teens with guitars, a girl with a flute, a boy on bongos and several singers. The kids led the audience in belting out upbeat renditions of "Blessed Assurance" and "O For A Thousand Tongues To Sing." Then everyone made a mad scramble for the various classrooms. To Noelle's relief, Gus left to help supervise the kids' crafts—something suitable for his maturity level. Her parents went upstairs to the Marriage and Family Class. She headed for the discussion group that was held in a cubbyhole beside the boiler room, making this room the hottest spot in the building.

A circle of folding chairs had been set up in the small space. Noelle grabbed the seat farthest away from the leader and slipped her raincoat over the back of her chair. The other group members, most holding Styrofoam cups of coffee or tea, trickled in, including the mayor (his wife went to choir practice); May Wells, a nurse; Trevor Spellman, a reporter from the *Yuletide Herald*; Edna Apple, a schoolteacher, and Julia Beems. The members greeted one another, removed their wraps, and took their seats. Noelle pulled a memo book and sharpened pencil from her purse. Tonight she was preoccupied with the mission, not the discussion. Doodling would help keep her anxiety at bay.

The discussion leader started the ball rolling. "Tonight we're going to look at the factors causing the rising crime rate across the nation."

A murdered man had collapsed in Noelle's living room, and the last thing she wanted to talk about was more violence. She drew flowers and birds in her memo book as the leader read some dry statistics about criminal activity in Indianapolis and Fort Wayne. A couple of people commented on how Yuletide was fairly safe, save for the bully boys with their loud motorcycles and the drunks outside the Tipsy Tavern.

May Wells was due on her hospital shift later that evening, so she was already wearing her white uniform dress, minus the cap. "What about the young man who was shot and died last Saturday?"

Noelle dropped her pencil. She leaned over and fumbled under her chair until she found the elusive writing tool, stuffing it and the memo book back in her purse. The conversation had grabbed her full attention.

"You must be mistaken." Christopher Kloss gave a patronizing grin. "Nobody's been shot lately."

"You're wrong." May shook her head so hard her beehive threatened to tumble off her scalp. "Last Saturday I was working the night shift. The ambulance brought in a man with a gunshot wound to his chest. It was all very hush-hush."

"Why wasn't I informed?" Trevor Spellman, a bit of a rebel with collar-length red hair and sideburns, was dressed in a turtleneck sweater and dark bell-bottoms. "The hospital is supposed to report all deaths to the paper so we can run an obit."

"The man had no identification on him," said the mayor. "You can't write an obit about a stranger."

"And how do you know this?" The reporter pulled a pad and pen from his pants pocket, clicked the ballpoint, and poised the pen over a blank page.

"I'm the mayor! I'm supposed to know what's going on in town."

"And keep it hidden from the public?" Trevor's hand twitched, itching to write some news.

Chris sputtered. "We didn't want to alarm the citizens. One death is hardly a crime wave."

"A man is murdered, and you think it isn't news?"

"It was probably a suicide."

The nurse said, "The man was shot in the chest." She pointed a finger at her chest, not realizing she was drawing attention to her ample bosom. "Suicides don't shoot themselves in the chest."

The spinster schoolteacher furrowed her brow. "Who was this young man? Was he a tourist? Did someone try to rob him? This is very distressing."

Chris smiled and held out his hands. "I assure you, the streets of Yuletide are the safest in the nation. Nobody here is going to be robbed or shot on his way home tonight. This was just an unfortunate incident."

Trevor asked, "Have the police caught the shooter?"

Julia Beems sat with her legs crossed and her hands perched atop her knees, left hand on top. She twisted her hand to catch the overhead lighting and make the diamond in her engagement ring sparkle for all to see. "Not with Chief Whitlock on the case. He couldn't catch a cold."

"Excuse me!" The group leader raised his hand and his voice. "I think we're getting off track here. I have some prepared discussion questions—"

"You want to talk about crime," said Trevor, "and we have a murder right here in our town!"

The group disintegrated into bedlam, with each person in the circle turning to his neighbor and stating an opinion about the shooting, the prices at the grocery store or the high school basketball game last Friday. Trevor grabbed the seat of his chair and scooted over to the mayor, peppering him with questions. Chris rose as a blush spread across in his face beyond his usual rosy cheeks. He grabbed his coat and stormed into the hallway with the reporter on his heels. The group leader gave up and stuck his lesson outline into a notebook.

The schoolteacher asked, "So what happened to the poor man who was shot?"

"The body was taken away," said May. "That's all I know."

Noelle joined the conversation. "Did you see who

took the body?"

"He was young, dark hair, skinny. He spoke in a low voice. His face looked pretty ordinary. That's what I remember most. He was so average my eyes kept sliding off him. Nothing special to hold my attention."

That sounds like Dash Hanover, Noelle thought, or maybe all SIAMESE agents had the ability to vanish.

"How awful to die and not have any family present," said Edna.

Noelle's cheeks burned. Should she tell them the victim's name? He wasn't just a John Doe—he was somebody. But she'd be bombarded with questions as to how she knew the man. Hanover and Chris both had ordered her to keep the incident under wraps, but was that the right thing to do? If she kept quiet, would she be helping or hindering a murder investigation?

Someone walked through the hallway, clanging one of the large bells from the handbell choir, the signal for the groups to wrap it up for the night. That got Noelle off the hook—for now. But could she look her neighbors in the eye tomorrow and stay quiet?

"That was some class tonight, wasn't it, Noelle?"

The question started her. Edna was standing over her.

Noelle quickly picked up her purse, put on her raincoat, and tried to think of something intelligent to say as she and her friend left the room. "Yes, yes it was."

"I'm surprised you didn't say anything."

Noelle's eyes grew wide. "What do you mean?"

"Usually you're pretty talkative, always jumping in with your opinion."

"I had nothing to share." Why did she find it so easy to lie to a friend?

"Do you think it was the work of a serial killer?" Edna said. "I read these true-crime magazines, and this month's issue had an article about a pervert who broke into the bedrooms of women and he—"

"The man who died in Yuletide wasn't in a bedroom, and he didn't attack women. Why do you read those trashy magazines anyway? They make up that stuff just to get people excited. None of it is true."

"Really?"

May joined them. "If the guy was a stranger, what was he doing in Yuletide in the first place? People don't come here to die."

Why did everyone want to yak about the one topic Noelle yearned to avoid? She checked her watch—Destiny should be here to pick her up. She had to find an excuse to leave. The friends reached the fellowship hall and ambled into the kitchen where some of the older ladies were packing up the leftover food from the potluck. The trio swiped a handful of cookies from an open container.

Edna said, "Do you think it was an accident? Maybe the man was cleaning a gun and it went off? Like the time a farmer was killed when one of his kids drove over him with a tractor."

May replied, "I saw the man in the hospital. I'd definitely say it was murder."

The kitchen crew eyed them, so the threesome moved into a dark corner of the fellowship hall, near the rack that stored the various ribbons won by the congregation's Boy Scout troop.

"Murder is a sin," said Edna. "I can't imagine how someone could do that."

"I can," said May. "My friend Vickie swears she's going to kill—" She lowered her voice as the other two huddled close. "Back in college, one of my sorority sisters and I spent the summer with my aunt and uncle in Riverbend. My sister met this guy. He seemed real nice and all. Had a thing for blondes. Anyway, he took her out on a date and they, you know, did it. Vickie got preggers, and the guy ran off. He wouldn't speak to her or answer her phone calls. Her parents had a fit and sent her off to an unwed mothers' home."

Edna said, "Wow! Did she keep the baby?"

"No. Her parents made her give it up for adoption. I think she wanted to keep it. Vickie says if she ever catches that guy, she's going to kill him."

"How is she going to find him?" the teacher asked. "Did he tell her his name?"

"He sure did. Kent Calvert."

The revelation surprised Noelle so much that she let the cookies slide out of her hands. She bent over to pick them up.

"Eww, don't eat those now," said Edna. "They've been on the floor."

"Yeah, you're right." Noelle dropped the treats into a nearby trashcan. "Has Vickie seen this Kent Calvert since the baby was born?"

"I don't think so. But who knows. She lives in Indy, and she doesn't tell me everything she does."

Noelle glanced at the wall clock. "That's an interesting story. I hate to run, but I gotta go. I, um, I have to go home and feed the cat. 'Bye, girls."

As the friends gave her puzzled looks, Noelle ran up the back stairs. Outside she took a deep breath of the cool, crisp night air to clear her head. A pair of headlights flashed. Noelle didn't hear an engine, so the vehicle must be one of the SIAMESE cars from the parking garage. The car was so black she could hardly see it in the darkness. As she hurried to the car, the front passenger door swung open and she slid in. The door automatically shut once she was seated. Good thing she didn't have an arm or leg sticking out.

"You're late." Destiny tapped her long, red-painted fingernails on the steering wheel. She had changed from her bright orange jumpsuit into a long-sleeved navy blouse and bell-bottoms, more suitable for nighttime prowling, along with an open black leather jacket.

"Sorry, I—"

"Our assignments run on split-second timing. Hesitation can kill you."

Using the gear lever on the steering column, Destiny shifted the car from park into drive and stomped on the accelerator.

Noelle braced herself. "Watch it! There's a speed limit in town!"

"We know about the cops in Yuletide. They're as useful as an empty tank of gas at a tractor pull."

Traffic was light, and Destiny hit the four-lane state highway to Riverbend at ten miles over the posted speed limit.

"The car's rigged with a warning system," said Destiny. "If a cop gets interested in us, I'll slow down."

The dashboard didn't resemble any that Noelle had seen. Every inch of the panel had a button or lever that operated a function. Lights flashed, and updated data continually scrolled on a small screen.

Destiny glanced at her. "Seatbelt."

"Oh, yeah." Noelle found the belt and buckled it across her lap. "Anyway, I'm sorry I was late, but I heard some wild news about Kent Calvert. Do you know about him? The guy who got shot and came to my house?"

"Yeah, Hanover told me." Destiny didn't sound interested. She kept her eyes glued to the road ahead.

Noelle shared what she knew about Kent's relationships with Gus and Vickie. "So at least two people knew Kent and had a reason to kill him."

"Child, you've been reading too many mystery books. People make threats all the time, but put a gun in their hand and they turn to mush."

"Don't you think we should check on them?"

"We cats at SIAMESE are spies, not detectives. We handle information, not whodunits."

"But these people have motives."

"What you need is evidence, not feelings."

Destiny shoved an eight-track cartridge into the player beneath the dash. From the hi-fi quad speakers came the sounds of "Baby Doll" by The Supremes.

After a mile of music, Noelle asked, "Why did you become a spy?"

"'Cause I didn't want to work as a maid."

"Do you like working with Dash Hanover? He's so gruff."

"Don't let him fool you. Beneath that suit of armor he's a pussycat. He acts tough 'cause if anything goes wrong, it all comes down on his head. The CIA hates us 'cause we get the job done faster, cheaper and better. They're looking for any excuse to lop off his head and shut us down."

"Why don't you work together with the CIA?"

Destiny laughed as they drove past The Star drive-in theater, which was closed for the winter. "You mean CIA as in Clumsy, Inefficient and Asinine. They wouldn't recognize a spy if he rang the doorbell and said howdy. We cats work better on our own."

"Have you ever been captured by the enemy?"

"Yeah."

"What happened?"

Destiny cast a sideways glance at her passenger. "You really don't want to know."

Chapter 14: What's New, Pussycat?

Even the glow of the streetlights couldn't brighten the drabness of the Riverbend downtown area that stretched along the northern banks of the Ohio River. The once-teeming business and retail district had deteriorated after World War 2 ended, and young families fled to the new suburban homes on the outskirts of town. With mostly lower-income single people now living downtown, the family-centered businesses had closed or moved out, leaving in their wake adult-oriented fare like cigar and liquor stores, greasy spoon diners, tattoo parlors and nightclubs.

Destiny maneuvered skillfully through the narrow one-way streets. She backed into an alley with the front grill facing the street, and parked along the right-hand side between a fire hydrant and a large trash bin.

"So nobody can block us in. We can make a fast getaway," she explained. "Take off your necklace and put it in your handbag. You can't wear anything with your name or initials." Destiny handed Noelle a brown clutch attached to a shoulder strap made of a thin cord. "Put your makeup and a hanky in here. I'll lock your bag in the car."

"Why can't I use my own purse?"

"'Cause the security might be lousy. Some clown might poke around and see your name and address on your driver's license."

That made sense. Noelle transferred her cosmetics and a handful of Kleenex, things that wouldn't matter if they were stolen, to the smaller bag.

Destiny placed Noelle's purse into the glove compartment and locked it. "Your name's Sue Smith. Got that?"

"Isn't Smith a little obvious as an alias?"

"Lots of people are named Smith. And I'm Dinah Jackson."

Destiny punched a dashboard button—both front doors popped open. Noelle stepped into a mound of cigarette butts discarded from various car ashtrays. She lifted her foot and shook off the clinging ashes. Destiny joined her outside. The car doors closed on their own and locked.

"Don't you have a key to the car?" Noelle asked.

"Keys are clunky. The car opens with this"—she showed Noelle a black clicker—"and starts when I press the ignition button with my thumb. The car reads my thumbprint so it knows I'm not a car thief."

"That's amazing. My little Bug doesn't do all that."

"Your life doesn't depend on what your little Bug can do." Destiny dropped the clicker into her own small purse.

Noelle slung the clutch strap over her shoulder. "For such a little bag, it's heavy."

"There's a metal bulletproof plate sewn in between the fabric layers. If someone takes a pot shot at you, use your bag as a shield. And when we reach the target, I do all the talking. Got it? You just tag along like a good little girl."

Noelle fumed at Destiny's attitude, but said nothing. Why did SIAMESE want her along if they didn't want her to do anything? Noelle couldn't see much in the dimly lit alley, but she could smell the piles of rotting garbage. The actress gingerly stepped around stacks of discarded, broken furniture. She jumped as a rat scampered past; Ceebee would enjoy chasing the rodent. A light drizzle fell.

Destiny sneezed. "Bless you," said Noelle.

"This cruddy weather. That's what I get for working nights." Destiny took a hanky from her purse and blew her nose.

They reached the backstage entrance to the Funky Feline Club. Destiny knocked, and a panel slid open in the door. Two bloodshot eyes gazed through the peephole.

A gruff voice said, "Whaya want?"

Destiny said, "We're the dancers for tonight."

"Yeah?" The eyes scanned the women. "You don't look like dancers."

"Let us in. We get our pay docked if we're late."

"You sure you ain't cops?"

Destiny changed tactics. She spoke sweetly and began to slowly unbutton her blouse. "Now, sugar, do I look like a cop to you?"

The eyes on the other side of the door grew large. As Destiny continued opening her blouse, the peephole closed and the door opened. "Come on in, toots."

As the spies crossed threshold, Noelle sucked in her breath. The burly guy was large, but the bulk consisted of muscle, not fat. His arms could easily snap a board in two. If this gorilla threw a punch, her little purse couldn't stop it.

"Dressing room's last door on the right." The doorman swatted Destiny on her rear. "Hey, baby, after you finish tonight I could use me some brown sugar."

She held her blouse closed with one hand and gave him a sickeningly sweet smile. But as the women walked down the hall, Destiny's smile turned into a scowl. She muttered something awful about the bouncer.

Noelle whispered, "Good thing he let us in when he did, or you might have run out of buttons."

"A creep like that wouldn't know what to do if I

did."

Like everything about the nightclub, the dressing room was a pitiful sight. Rusted, dented metal lockers stood on a dusty floor. An odor of stale cigarettes and beer filled the changing room. Noelle held her breath and made a super-fast pit stop in the dirty restroom. Next to the cracked wall mirror stood a metal clothes rack. Destiny flipped through the offerings and pulled out a particular wire hanger holding an outfit.

"This looks like your size." She handed it to Noelle. "Put it on."

Noelle hung her raincoat in one of the lockers and sat on a creaky wooden bench to change into the clothes: pink tights, a low-cut pink leotard with long sleeves, and mid-calf go-go boots made of shiny white plastic. Atop her head went a plastic headband with a pair of pink fabric cat ears. She slipped on white gloves with long golden "claws" on the fingertips. Noelle studied her reflection in the mirror and fingered the pink tail that dangled from the backside of the leotard.

"Am I supposed to go out in public like this? I look more like a hooker than a cat."

Destiny's costume was the same, except in gold with black gloves and boots. "You're an actress. It's your costume."

"If my mom saw me in this, she'd have a heart attack."

Someone pounded on the door. "You girls ready?" The voice came from a throat burned raw by cigarettes.

"Yes, sir, we'll be right out," Destiny said to Noelle, "Hang up your clothes, Sue Smith. It's show time."

Noelle stuffed her street clothes and purse into the locker and shut the door. "There's no lock on the door. How do I keep people from stealing my clothes?"

"You don't."

Someone gave three loud raps on the door. Without

waiting for a reply, a man with a broken nose and hair like a Brill-O pad opened the door. His wrinkled white shirt and brown suit and trousers would be rejected if he tried to donate them to the Salvation Army. He reeked of cheap aftershave.

He ran his puffy eyes over the spies. "I'm Mr. Squall, the manager. You're the best the agency could send me?"

Destiny shrugged. "It's a busy night. Everybody else is working."

He sighed. "If the customers are drunk, maybe they won't notice. Come on, girls."

They moved down the narrow corridor single file with Mr. Squall in front, Destiny in the middle and Noelle tagging in the rear. She tugged at the hem of the leotard that kept creeping up her backside. The man opened a door and the club sucked them into a vortex of sight, sound and smell.

Music from the rock trio of guitar, bass and drums pounded from the wall amps. The bands at The Barn were loud, but never like this. If the band was playing a Top 40 hit, Noelle couldn't hear the melody over the heavy bass. The shaggy-haired band, playing from a platform squeezed against one wall, was barely visible beneath the dim lighting and a haze of cigarette smoke. Rows of tiny colored lights embedded in the ceiling blinked in random patterns. A hidden projector beamed hypnotic swirls of light onto the white walls. On either side of the band platform stood the pillars, each topped with a tall gold cage. Mr. Squall motioned for Noelle to climb the steps that circled the column. She gamely took the steps, which had no handrail to keep her from plummeting to the floor, and he followed.

At the top of the column, the manager gestured at the cage. "Get in."

She swallowed and stepped into the narrow cage.

Even though the cage had bars instead of solid walls, Noelle felt closed in. Mr. Squall pulled a key ring from his pocket and locked the door.

Noelle shook the bars of the door. "You will let me out of here, won't you?"

"When it's time for your break. Had too many girls get lazy and quit halfway into their shifts. Now shake your tush and look sexy."

As Mr. Squall descended the steps, Noelle gave a wane smile. Finding the beat of the loud music wasn't hard, although the volume was giving her a headache. After five minutes of frantic dancing she slowed down. She had to conserve her energy, or she wouldn't last. To her left she saw Destiny jiving in the other cage. They were too far away to talk. To keep her mind occupied, Noelle examined the patrons seated at the tables. The room was one-quarter filled, mostly with couples sitting and talking or staring numbly at the band. Waitresses dressed in the cat leotards roamed the floor, dispensing drinks from metal trays. With the smoke hanging in the air, she couldn't see faces clearly. Where was the contact? Noelle hoped he'd show up soon. She couldn't tolerate an entire night trapped in the cage. The smoke made her cough. At least her job at the park was out in the clean air. Noelle passed the time by daydreaming of working in Hollywood as a go-go dancer on the TV show *Shindig*, where she might someday stand close to a groovy rock star or teen idol.

At long last Mr. Squall arrived and unlocked the cage door. "Ten-minute break."

Noelle nodded and stepped out of the cage, feeling woozy from the smoke and noise. Her cramped legs carefully took the steps. Once on the floor, she leaned back and massaged her aching waist. If she didn't get some water soon, her throat would turn into the Sahara Desert. The sweaty leotard and tights clung uncomfortably tight.

Destiny stepped up to Noelle and spoke softly. "Bulldog's here, back corner table at eleven o'clock."

"But it's only ten-thirty."

"I don't mean the time, I mean direction as a clock hand points. Never mind."

Noelle started to move toward the table, but Destiny grabbed her arm and pulled her behind the pillar, out of view of the patrons. "You can't come with me."

"Why not?"

"Bulldog might freak out with two people ganging up on him. You sit at that table beside him."

"Why?"

Destiny sounded exasperated. "The people at that table arrived when Bulldog did. They haven't budged. They may be tailing him. You need to distract them while I make contact."

"What do I say to them?"

"You're an actress. Improvise."

Destiny gave Noelle a push that nearly knocked her off her sore feet. Noelle recovered, smoothed her hair and headed toward the table. Her heart pounded as loudly as the music. Surely the patrons would see straight through her disguise. What if something happened to her? How would she explain to her mother how she ended up inside such a weird nightclub?

Two couples sat at the table. The two women and one of the men were laughing loudly. The other man gave Noelle the hairy eyeball. He rested his elbows on the table and held a lit cigarette. His purple Nehru jacket looked expensive. Noelle approached. No backing out now. She had to get into character. She put on a huge grin and swiveled her hips to look charming, but instead nearly put her hip socket out of joint.

"Hey, big guy, can I sit at your table?"

The man didn't blink as he ran his eyes over her.

"Now why would you want to do that?"

"'Cause you look like a pretty groovy bunch of swingers."

"You think so?" He sounded annoyed.

The young woman seated beside the man tapped his arm. "Let the chick sit. She'd be a lot more laughs than you are, you dreary old windbag." Despite the cool weather outside, the gal with the long stringy hair wore a sleeveless miniskirt and no coat.

The man turned his head just enough to direct his next line to his tablemate. "If you don't like my company, get lost."

"Stop being such a drag." The woman smiled at Noelle and patted the empty stool beside her. "Hey, you, sit over here with me and help take my mind off old sourpuss."

The man cast a sideways glance at the woman. He gulped down the last dregs of his drink and watched the other customers. He ignored Noelle, who slid onto the stool, teetering unsteadily on the narrow seat. The other man and woman at the table were engaged in their own conversation and paid her scant attention.

The woman slipped her hands around Noelle's arm. "I like you. I'm Dixie." She had a pronounced Southern accent like someone from Kentucky. The smell of alcohol hung on her breath. "What's your name?"

Noelle stiffened. She wasn't used to strangers getting so familiar, so fast. What was the alias Destiny wanted her to use? "I'm Sue. Sue Smith"

"Hello, Sue. How do you do." Dixie giggled at her joke. She slapped the man in the Nehru jacket on the arm. "Be a gentleman and order the girl a drink. What's your poison, Sue?"

"A root beer, please."

"Root beer? That's for baby bottles. I mean a drink for grown-ups."

Noelle eyed the empty shot glasses littering the table. Coming from a family of teetotalers, she wouldn't know a vintage red wine from a sloe gin fizz. What could she say that didn't sound stupid?

"I'll have whatever you're having."

Dixie tugged the man's sleeve. "Order some drinks—what did you say your name was?"

He didn't look at her. "I didn't."

The man motioned for a waitress to come and take his order. While they waited for the drinks to arrive, Dixie rambled on about something or the other, but Noelle barely listened. She nodded politely but kept an eye on the other table where Destiny was deep in conversation with a lone man who looked like the guy on the slide shown in the briefing room. Noelle hoped they would finish their business soon so she could escape before the drinks arrived—but too late. A waitress set several glasses on the table. Noelle stared at the scotch on the rocks in front of her. She'd never even tasted liquor before, let alone downed an entire glass.

"Cheers!" Dixie raised her glass. "Come on, bottom's up." She and the other couple clinked their glasses. The man in the Nehru jacket didn't touch his glass, as he seemed more interested in Destiny's conversation with Bulldog. Noelle lifted her glass to her lips and watched as Dixie knocked back hers. Noelle smiled and set her glass on the table, hoping the others wouldn't notice it was still full. If Dixie was a spy, she didn't act the part, unless her drunkenness was part of an act.

At the other table, Bulldog rose and headed for a back door. Destiny left the table as well, moving toward the dressing room. Time for Noelle to exit—but how to depart gracefully?

"I need to make a phone call." The man in the Nehru jacket took a quick sip of his fresh Manhattan and left.

"I should go too." Noelle started to stand, but Dixie grabbed her arm and pulled her down.

"Don't go yet, the party's just starting. Now that Mr. Giggles is gone, we'll have some real fun." Dixie fished around in her purse and pulled out a huge joint. She picked up a lighter from the tabletop and lit up. Noelle fought the urge to fan away the fumes.

Dixie handed the joint to the actress. "Here you go. Guests first. Have a toke."

Chapter 15: Runaway

Noelle starred at the pot stick. According to the movies shown in the high school personal hygiene class, teens turned into raving lunatics after one puff of marijuana. But if she didn't smoke, she'd blow her cover. The others at the table eyed her.

"Hurry up," said the other man. "The rest of us want a hit too."

The full drink on the table gave her an idea. Noelle reached for the joint, but deliberately brushed her hand against the glass and knocked it onto her lap. She squealed in genuine shock and sprang to her feet as the ice cubes and cold liquor slid down her legs.

"Icky, icky! I gotta to go to the bathroom and clean up."

Dixie handed her a cloth napkin from the table. "Oh, Sue, don't be a baby. Wipe it off and sit down."

"No, really, if I ruin this outfit, I gotta pay for it." Goofy, but it was the best excuse she could dream up on short notice. "Excuse me."

Before her tablemate could protest, Noelle hurried off and met up with Destiny in the ladies' dressing room. Her partner had her jacket on and purse in hand.

"Put on your coat. We gotta go." Destiny shoved Noelle's raincoat and clutch into her hands. "The contact is meeting us in the alley right now. He's being watched."

"Sure, as soon as I clean up—"

"No time."

"But, Destiny, I smell like a brewery!"

"Take a bath when you get home."

Before Noelle had a chance to even slip on her raincoat, Destiny grabbed her wrist and pulled her into the hallway—right into the beefy stomach of the manager.

"Hey!" he said. "Break's over! You girls get your hinnies back in those cages!"

"We took a job at the club down the street," said Destiny. "Pay's better."

"I got a contract—"

"So tear it up."

The spies raced down the hall.

"Hey! Wait a minute! There ain't no club down the street!" Mr. Squall yelled at the doorman. "Stop those girls!"

The bruiser placed his bulk between the women and the back door. He held up his fists, ready to rumble. Noelle caught her breath and stopped, but Destiny met the man head on. She stopped and twisted her body so her right side faced him. She gave a short yell of power. Her right leg shot out and the sole of her foot kicked the guy hard in his unprotected gut. He lowered his hands to cradle his tummy. Destiny turned and faced him head on. Her right hand pulled back to counter balance as her left fist shot out and punched his face. He staggered back, holding his bloody nose.

"Come on!" Destiny pulled Noelle into the alley.

Outside, Noelle breathed deeply of the night air. The faint tang of the salty river water and the stench of decomposing garbage smelled like roses compared to the club's atmosphere. Rain was falling, so Noelle put on her coat and buttoned it. Destiny pulled a thin flashlight from her purse and switch it on.

"Where did you learn to fight like that?" Noelle asked.

"Tae kwon do black belt, and keep your voice

down." Destiny swept the light around them. "He said he'd be here."

A cloud hid the moon. The streetlights couldn't cut through the drizzle. Noelle couldn't see a thing. Two gunshots rang through the alley. Destiny moved in the direction of the shots. Noelle followed. After a few feet, the black woman stopped and held up her hand. She pointed her flashlight at a man lying face down on the ground. The spy squatted, rolled the body over, and shone the beam into his face. Bulldog's eyes stared back but saw nothing. Two bullet holes punched his bloody chest. Noelle put her hands to her mouth to keep from screaming. She'd only seen dead bodies at funeral homes, gussied up for a viewing. Those poor souls had died of natural causes at home, not from a killer in a dank alley.

From the distance came the wail of a police siren.

Destiny stared in the direction of the sound. "Noelle, quick, search the pockets on his left side. I'll do the right. We gotta scram before the cops get here."

"You want me to touch a dead body?"

Destiny sounded impatient. "No, just his pockets. We're not stripping him."

"What am I looking for?"

"I don't know! Anything you find, stuff it in your purse. We'll look at it later. Hurry!"

The siren grew louder. The women pulled off the clumsy cat gloves and tossed them into the trash bin. Noelle knelt beside the body and wiped the rainwater off her face so she could see. She gingerly poked her hand into the man's pockets, trying her best not to look directly into the ashen face. Destiny moved rapidly, shoveling the man's belongings into her open handbag. A police car turned into the far end of the alley. The bubblegum light atop the car roof flashed red. Destiny switched off her flashlight. The women crouched and scooted to the side of the alley, hiding behind a huge metal trash bin, out of sight of the headlights—but for how long? As the cop car inched along the passage, the tires squished the mud and garbage. The cruiser stopped in front of the body. Noelle held her breath and didn't move. Two beat cops left the car and shone their flashlights on the dead man. As the men talked among themselves, the women slipped along the wall toward their car. One cop returned to his car, opened the front door and reached inside for the radio receiver to call in. His back was to the spies. Just a few more feet to the car—and Noelle kicked a tin can. The clatter sounded like a thunderclap.

The cop with the radio turned his head. "Stop! Who's there?"

Destiny reached into her bag, removed the car clicker, and pushed a button. The front doors on the car swung open. "Duck and run!"

As the police reached for their guns, the women sprang into the car. The car doors shut as their rears hit the seats. Destiny pressed the ignition button on the console. The engine revved. She stomped the accelerator. The car lunged forward. Noelle braced herself against the dashboard as Destiny raced through the streets, taking every turn at top speed. When raindrops hit the windshield, the sensors automatically switched on the wipers. After several minutes of erratic driving, she slowed the car.

Destiny checked her rearview mirror. "We lost them." She headed for the highway on two-lane residential streets, avoiding the major thoroughfares.

Noelle fastened her seat belt and sank back into the seat. "I'm exhausted. I can't wait to get home and into a warm bath."

"You'll have to wait. We're spending the night at the safe house."

"The what?"

"We can't stay on the road. If the cops call in a description of the car, every flatfoot in the county will be looking for us. SIAMESE keeps a safe house outside of town. We can wait there until the coast is clear."

"But I want to go home now."

"We can't. Something's wrong."

"I'd say there is. There's a dead man back there."

"You got that right, sister. Agents don't kill contacts. Too messy. Leaves a trail and the cops start snoopin' around. Even if Bulldog double-crossed the Reds, they wouldn't leave a stiff lying around in public. And the pros use silencers."

"So who killed the contact? A hobo on the street looking for money?"

"How many bums do you know own a pistol?" Destiny sniffed. "Speaking of bums, you smell like a tramp with a hip flask of whisky that broke in his pants."

Noelle rubbed her arms. "Yeah, and I'm freezing, too."

Destiny pressed the heater button. The car quickly filled with warm air. "We'll get you cleaned up soon. I can't turn in this car with it stinking like a cheap dive."

"Hey, I just remembered. My clothes are still in the locker. We have to go back to the club."

"Dash should have warned you. Don't wear your best outfit on a mission. Sometimes we leave things behind."

"Rats!"

They turned onto an empty back road that wound past acres of farmland.

"But we have more important issues than your threads," said Destiny. "We got a wild card on our hands."

"A what?"

"Whoever killed Bulldog wasn't a Russian agent. Killing contacts is not their style. This new guy may be an independent out to sell the microdot to the highest bidder. Or he wants to take on Bulldog's identity so he can pass on fake info. Whoever he is, he's bad news. We know how the Russians think, but a wild card's unpredictable."

"So what do we do?"

"Get the microdots before World War III breaks out."

"Well, if that's all . . . " Noelle stared out the side window at the fields rushing by. "I hope Ceebee gets fed in the morning."

They drove down a dirt path and into a grove of trees. The road ended at a clearing with only a barn covered in peeling paint and weather-beaten boards.

Noelle felt grumpy and hungry. "I thought we were going to a safe house."

"We are."

"Where is it?"

Destiny nodded at the barn. "Right there."

"That creepy old shack?"

Destiny pressed yet another button on the dashboard. A panel in the side of the barn swung upward. The car coasted inside the building. The door closed. Overhead lights snapped on, revealing a spotlessly clean garage. To the left, a metal wall with a single door ran the length of the garage. The women took their purses and left the car. Destiny pressed a passcode into the wall pad. The door opened. She stepped inside, turned on a switch that operated the lights and heat, and motioned for Noelle to follow.

"Wow!" Noelle exclaimed. "What a nifty apartment!"

The room was comfortably furnished with a sofa, a square wooden table with four matching chairs, a kitchenette and doors leading to a bedroom and a bath. What made the windowless room different from the average home was the bank of monitors and computer equipment. Destiny flipped a switch on the equipment. The screens flickered on, showing views from the exterior security cameras. The buttons on the computer panel lit up, and the machinery gave a soft purring sound.

Noelle eyed it with excitement. "I would have never guessed this was inside that crummy old barn."

"That's the idea. Anyone chasing us would get the same idea. Are you hungry?"

"I'm famished."

"Whatever we eat is out of a can. Can't keep fresh food in here, what with people in and out at odd hours."

"Right now I don't care if you cut pictures of food out of a magazine and fried them. But I need to get out of this stinky outfit. Do you have a shower in this place?"

Destiny pointed to one of the doors. "In there."

Inside the bathroom, Noelle peeled off the sweat-and-alcohol soaked costume as well as her undies. What a relief to get rid of that silly cat getup. The room was equipped with soap, shampoo, towels, combs, razors, shaving cream, and toothbrushes. Everything a spy on the run might need. A quick shower washed off the dirt and stink. Then she realized something.

Noelle tapped on the door. "Hey, Destiny. I don't have any clean clothes. What am I going to wear?"

"Come on out and we'll get you fixed up."

Noelle glanced around the room. The bath towels were not large enough to use as a cover up. But the bathtub had an opaque shower curtain. She unhooked the sheet of plastic from the rod rings and wrapped the crinkly curtain around her. Noelle held it firmly in place as she stepped out of the bathroom.

Destiny laughed. "Don't be such a prude! No one's gonna see you. It's just us girls in here."

Noelle blushed. She'd always been shy about her body. Back in high school, she hated stripping before her classmates in the dressing room for P.E. classes. Maybe it was the fact she'd never grown bigger than the smallest B cup. Now she just felt awkward trying to hold up the cumbersome curtain.

"You look like a mummy. Here." Destiny paused in her kitchen duties long enough to open a closet door. "This is our clothes stash. We're always getting our rags messed up. Help yourself."

"Gosh, thanks. It's just for tonight."

"Keep it. We're always restocking. You can change in the bedroom. I promise not to peek."

In the closet Noelle found a red, long-sleeved flannel shirt (roomy), gray slacks (snug) and black loafers The bedroom contained two twin beds, two chairs, a bureau and some folding cots stacked in a corner. Just how many people stayed in here at one time?

"Destiny, what about underwear?"

"In the dresser."

Noelle rummaged in the drawers and couldn't find bras in her size, so she settled for a man's white undershirt along with the white panties and black socks. After she dressed, the aroma of fresh-brewed coffee lured her back into the main room.

"That coffee smells great!"

"I figured you could use some. Unless you'd rather have a scotch."

"No, thanks. I'll stick with the coffee."

Destiny shrugged. "Suit yourself."

The spy poured a cup of coffee from the stainless-steel percolator and handed it to her partner. At the fully stocked bar she fixed a scotch and soda for herself. Noelle found paper plates in a cupboard and plastic cutlery in a drawer. She set the table. Destiny served the food. Each plate had toast along with fried slices of Spam and powdered eggs scrambled and mixed with diced tomatoes from a can.

"It ain't haute cuisine, but it's filling."

"It smells great, Destiny. Yum!"

"Cookies and snack cakes are in the cabinet."

"Before we eat, can you do me a favor?"

"What?"

"Take off the goofy cat suit. It looks stupid."

"Thanks, kid. I get busy thinking about our next move to remember what I'm wearing. Here." She handed Noelle a can opener. "Pick out some fruit."

Destiny opened the clothes closet and tore off the costume, not at all shy about dressing in the open. Noelle turned her back and busied herself with the food. She opened and poured a can of peaches into a serving bowl, and found a jar of peanut butter to spread on the toast. By the time she finished with the food, Destiny had changed into a form-fitting black turtleneck sweater and pants. They sat at the table. Destiny started eating, but Noelle bowed her head, folded her hands, and made a silent prayer. She raised her head to see her partner staring at her.

"You're something else." Destiny shook her head. "I never knew they grew girls so square down on the farm."

Noelle bristled. "I don't live on a farm. I reside in an agricultural community."

"So you say. You ever been outside of your little hick town?"

She got defensive. "I went to college in Terre Haute."

"Sister, don't you ever go to Chicago. They'd eat you alive."

Noelle seasoned her eggs with ample helpings of salt

and pepper and talked between bites. "Tell me about yourself. What do you do when you're not spying?"

Destiny cast her a dismissing glance. "I'd rather not."

"I was only trying to make small talk."

"Getting chummy with a partner is a bad idea. They might not be around the next day."

"Sorry. Have you ever lost a partner?"

"Yeah. Let's leave it at that." Destiny bent her face low over her plate so Noelle couldn't see her eyes welling up.

Noelle surmised that the spy was not only skilled at protecting state secrets but in also hiding facts about herself. "Have you worked with Dash Hanover a long time?"

"Long enough."

"I wouldn't want a boss like that."

"Why not? He's our best operator."

"Really? He's so mean to me."

"That's 'cause you're a civilian. He'd gotta be tough to make sure you come out of this alive."

"If he treated me a little better, I could go for him. Do agents ever date civilians?"

Density sent down her fork and stared at her. "Honey, you don't ever want to date Hanover. No way."

"Why not? Is he such a bad guy?"

"He's your cousin."

Chapter 16: Surprise, Surprise

The fork dropped from Noelle's hand and clattered on the table. "My cousin? That's a joke, right?"

"Hanover's mother is your mama's sister."

"My mom has two sisters, and I know all my cousins."

"You ever hear of the black sheep of the family? I'm talkin' 'bout the runt in your family flock. Next time you see your mama, ask her about your Auntie Grizelda."

"I don't have an aunt named Grizelda."

"Ye, you do. I don't jive 'bout things like that."

"How do you know?"

"Hanover told me. I don't like working with amateurs, but the big guy pushed for you 'cause you're family. He said you had the right genes. Now come on." Destiny got to her feet and began clearing the table. Her attitude turned to business. "HQ's waiting for my report, and then we're looking through those goodies we picked off the contact."

"Oh yeah, that."

Inside the cozy nest, the dark world of dead bodies and espionage seemed far away. The thick walls muffled the exterior sounds. The silent, flickering images on the monitors showed a raccoon roaming the grounds. Destiny washed the skillet and cooking utensils. Noelle threw away the disposable dishes. She was quiet, with her mind still reeling from the revelation of the new family member. Why the big mystery? Her mother never kept secrets from her.

"Let me ask you one more question," said Noelle.

"Shoot."

"Does Mr. Hanover have a family?"

"We all do, hon. None of us hatched out of an egg."

"Is Dash his real first name?"

"Yeah."

"Is Dash short for something?"

Destiny laughed. "If I told you his name, he'd demote me."

"Come on, what is it? I won't tell him you told me." Destiny shook her head. "Is it Dashell?" Another head shake. "Give me a hint."

"You were named for a holiday. Same with him."

"I was born on Christmas day. But Dash? What does that have to do with a holiday?"

"You think about it." The dishes finished, Destiny pulled out the rubber sink stopper and let the water drain. "Now shut up while I call HQ." She sat on a stool in front of the console of electronic equipment and turned on switches. She set up a microphone on the counter. "Black Manx calling Fido Brown."

After a moment, a speaker on the panel crackled with static, and lights flickered on a monitor until a black-and-white image of Hanover appeared. "Fido Brown here. What's your report?"

"Hi, Dash!" Noelle called from across the room. "It's me, Noelle."

A sigh of exasperation came over the speaker. "Will you tell your civilian partner we never use our real names during radio or phone communications?"

"Sorry," Noelle said.

"How was Tabby Gray's performance?" he asked.

"Satisfactory," Destiny replied.

Only satisfactory? For her first role of doing undercover work and looking at a dead body without fainting, Noelle thought she'd done pretty well. Destiny

gave her boss a brief rundown of their adventure at the
Funky Feline Club. When she described Bulldog's
death, the operative looked sad.

"He was a good contact," said Hanover. "That's a
shame to lose him. You saw no one else in the alley?"

"No, sir."

Noelle said, "I think I know who killed him."
Destiny glared at Noelle as she stepped up behind her
and leaned in close to the microphone. "At the club, a
man was watching Bulldog. He was sitting at the next
table. The guy wore a purple Nehru jacket. He followed
Bulldog out of the room. At the time I didn't think
anything about it because, well, I was busy with other
things."

"Lots of people were going in and out," Destiny
said.

"Yeah, I know, but this guy gave me the creeps.
Everyone else at the table was laughing and carrying
on, but this guy hardly said a word. He was so serious."

"Did he return to the table?" Hanover asked.

"I don't know. That's when Dest—Black Manx and
I left the club."

"Can you give us a description?"

"I think so."

"I'm putting you on hold while I put our sketch artist
on the line." The monitor went blank.

"Wow, this is exciting," said Noelle. "I might help
out after all."

"We'll see." Destiny didn't sound as enthused. "The
dude probably went out to use the john."

The monitor came back to life. A young man with a
Van Dyke beard held a drawing tablet and a pencil. He
sketched a face according to Noelle's description.
When he finished the drawing, he held it up before the
camera.

Noelle said, "That's him! That's that guy at the

table."

The artist nodded and stepped away. Hanover resumed his seat in front of the camera. "We'll run this picture through our database of enemy agents."

Destiny said, "Sir, we have a wild card on our hands. Bulldog's killer might be a new player."

"If that's true, then you girls be careful. And get Tabby Gray back home as soon as you can. If we have an unknown factor, we need to keep her involvement at a minimum."

He signed off, and Destiny powered down the radio. "All right, girl, time we go to work. Dump the stuff in your purse on the table and start looking for clues."

The agent freshened her scotch and soda at the bar, and Noelle poured herself another cup of coffee. Destiny set her drink on the table, opened her handbag, and removed a handgun.

Noelle stared at the weapon. "You had that on you all the time?"

"Right on. Agents never go into the field unarmed."

"If you had seen the guy who killed Bulldog, would you have shot him?"

The spy glared at her. "Come on, get busy."

Destiny poured the remaining contents of her bag onto the table. Noelle set down her coffee cup. She snapped open her clutch, turned it over, and let the contents drop. The women sat at the table and began sorting. They carefully examined the items gleaned from Bulldog's pockets. Noelle felt a little queasy pawing through the personal goods of a dead man, but she feared a nasty rebuttal from Destiny if she complained. The objects were typical of any man's pocket: coins, handkerchief, keys, comb, memo book, pen, folded city map, a newspaper clipping and a wallet holding bills and several driver's licenses in various names.

The spy picked up a small black cube, pressed a button on it, and held it over the objects. Off Noelle's puzzled look, she said, "It detects microdots that we might miss. Didn't have time to use it in the alley." But a thorough scan of the objects yielded nothing. Destiny turned off the device and set it down.

Noelle rested her chin on her fists. "Looks like the enemy got what they wanted after all."

"Don't think so. Spies don't kill contacts after they turn over the goods. They let them live another day so they can keep funneling data."

"Maybe Bulldog didn't want to give them what they wanted, so the guy shot him and took it."

"Contacts like to stay alive. They don't die for microdots. Doesn't matter to them who gets the information as long as they're paid."

"Maybe the microdot is—was on his clothes."

Destiny shook her head. "Too easy for a dot to get rubbed off. Let's go through this stuff one more time."

"Those keys. Maybe one of them opens a storage locker."

Destiny fingered the keys. "They're too big for locker keys. Besides, a key's something Bulldog could slip to me in the club. There's nothing suspicious about a guy giving a girl a key to his apartment." She set down the key ring. "HQ will run through the names on the licenses to match the aliases in our files. But he won't have his real name on any of them."

"What about the address book?"

"Spies don't carry around names and addresses unless they're coded."

Noelle picked up the clipping. "This is the only thing left. But why would he carry around a newspaper ad for soap?"

Destiny took the piece of paper and flipped it over. "It's an obit for a Mr. Otto Hildebrand."

"Maybe the spy gave the microdot to him."

"Don't think so. Says here Hildebrand was eighty-two years old when he died of cancer. A contact wouldn't give up information to a dying man."

"Maybe he was going to give the dot to someone at the funeral."

"The service was over a week ago. The obit says the guy lived in Riverbend. I'll drop by and see the next of kin. They might know if Hildebrand worked with intelligence. But first you need to go home."

"Go home? I'm not a kid out past curfew. I want to come with you."

"Your part of the mission is over."

"But I want to stay on. I've come this far. I want to find out what happens with Mr. Hildebrand and the microdot. It's like a TV show. I can't turn it off until I see the ending."

"I thought you wanted to go home."

Noelle smiled. "This is more exciting."

"Orders from HQ. You heard the big man. He wants you out of the picture for now. It's for your own safety."

"Come on, Destiny. This is the most challenging thing I've ever done. I was taught to always finish what I start. I'm not a quitter."

"Grab your coat and let's go."

"You said we couldn't leave until morning."

Destiny nodded at one of the outdoor monitors. "Morning has broken."

Sure enough, the rising sun was casting a warm glow in the east-facing camera. Noelle couldn't believe the night had passed and she'd gone this long without sleep. She'd been riding on adrenaline fumes all evening. But in the quiet of the safe house, the nervous tension oozed away. Her body just wanted to crash.

On the way to Yuletide, they listened to a morning

news report on the car radio. A brief blurb stated that a body had been found behind the Funky Feline Club. The police were interrogating the club owner, who denied any part in the murder.

Destiny said, "At least we got a scapegoat. It takes the heat off us."

Noelle said, "Yeah, but who *was* the killer?"

Chapter 17: Writer In The Sun
Thursday

The ring of the princess phone woke Noelle. She turned over in bed and glanced at the alarm clock. Almost noon. She snuggled back into bed, waiting for the caller to give up so she could catch some more zzzzzzs. But Destiny or Hanover could be calling with news about the mission. She stumbled out of bed, not taking time to put on a robe, and picked up the phone with a dazed "Hello?"

A man's voice answered, but not Hanover's. "Noelle? Is that you? You sound like you just got out of bed."

Drat. The nosey newspaper reporter was the last person she wanted to talk to. She cleared her throat and attempted to sound more alert. "No, I'm fine, Trevor. What do you want?"

"I need to talk to you about the death of Kent Calvert."

"Who?" With Bulldog's death, she had two murders juggling for space in her brain.

"You know who I'm talking about. My sources tell me an ambulance picked him up from your house Saturday night, and you came by the hospital to see him."

Trevor must have cozied up to the nurses at St. Nicholas. "Then you know as much about it as I do. Wait a minute. How did you find out his name?"

"Easy. I called my police contacts in the area and checked out any recent missing persons reports. I got a description of the deceased from May, and I found a name to match from the Riverbend files."

"Well, fiddle dee dee."

"Come on, Noelle, give me a break. This is the big scoop I've been waiting for. I'm sick to death of writing about the ladies' garden club and school bake sales. I finally got a hot news story I can sink my teeth into. It's my chance to move up to a bigger paper. Look, I've done some digging of my own, but I'm at a roadblock. Let's meet and compare notes. Maybe we can help each other."

Noelle rubbed her eyes. She'd rather crawl back into bed. "I don't know."

"I'm going to write this story with or without your help. I'd rather hear straight from you than rely on a secondhand source."

He had a point. Who knows what goofiness he'd hear from the townspeople. And if he'd gotten a whiff of SIAMESE, she needed to steer him in another direction.

Then he said the magic words. "Lunch is my treat."

"Okay, but not at The Igloo." She wasn't eager to deal with Vince or Gus E. Monty if either one showed up.

"North Pole Cafe?"

She agreed. Yuletide residents preferred the sit-down restaurant because it was classier than The Igloo, and they could avoid the tourists, who generally ate at the theme park. The cafe's food was nothing fancy, just good and filling home cooking served in huge portions for lunch and family style for dinner, topped with desserts to die for. She rifled through her closet for just the right clothes. With Trevor she could dress a little more daring than when she was around the uncool older folks. She settled on a charming schoolgirl outfit: plaid miniskirt with pleats, white long-sleeved blouse, black vest, red tie, nude hose and knee boots. As she was putting on her makeup, the phone rang again, this time from the Colonel. He had some information for her. She agreed to meet him late in the afternoon at one of his favorite haunts—and hers too—the public library.

At the restaurant, Noelle and Trevor hung their wraps on the coat stand and sat across from each other at a two-person table in a corner. In the center of the room stood the long wooden tables for groups and families. Except for a few retired couples, the two young people had the place to themselves. He ordered the breaded pork tenderloin sandwich, French fries and a Coke. She requested the hot ham and cheese sandwich, onion rings and root beer in a frosted mug. As the waitress in her white apron and red dress wrote down their orders, Noelle gazed at the wall mural of Mrs. Santa cooking a huge feast, and elves making candy in the North Pole kitchen. Perhaps she should have requested a restaurant in Riverbend, where one could find a place free of Christmas kitsch.

As the waitress headed for the kitchen, Trevor whipped out a steno pad and pen. "Okay, Noelle, tell me about Kent Calvert."

She stuck a straw into the glass of iced water that the waitress had left. "What's wrong with starting with 'hello, how are you?'"

"Sorry. I get wrapped up with my work. Hello, Noelle, how are you?"

"I'm fine, how are you?"

"I'm great. Now tell me about Kent Calvert."

"He came to my door, he fell on my floor, and he died the next day. That's what I know."

"You can do better than that. I called your house all day yesterday. Nobody answered. I called the record store and was told you never came to work. Your parents didn't know exactly where you were, and your mother is on top of everything that goes on in this town. If Mrs. McNabb is out of the loop, there's something rotten going on in Yuletide."

"I was in Riverbend shooting a TV commercial."

"What's the name of the production company?"

"I don't remember. I've sent headshots to every business in the county."

The waitress arrived with their food, putting a pause into the conversation. After she left, Noelle bit into the onion rings—greasy but oh so good.

Trevor continued, "Your mother said you were shooting a TV commercial. I called every advertising firm in Riverbend. Nobody had heard of you."

"It's a brand new company. They don't have a number yet, so they're not in the phone book."

"How did the company hire you if they couldn't call?"

Noelle became testy. "Why are you so snoopy? Why does it matter where I happened to be yesterday? What does that have to do with a dead man?" She raised her voice. "Am I under suspicion for murder?"

The other diners stared at them.

The reporter patted her hand and lowered his voice. "Relax, Noelle. Don't get huffy. This is your old buddy Trevor. We worked together on the high school yearbook, remember? We were in the school plays. I was your partner in biology lab when we cut up a frog and you nearly threw up. I'm not judging you, Noelle. I'm just trying to get the facts. I didn't work my tail off in four years of journalism school at I.U. to write about small town prom nights."

"Sorry, Trevor. This whole thing has me upset. Why haven't you talked to Chief Whitlock? Seems like he's the one who should know about this case."

"I have, and he doesn't. He assumes a vagrant shot Calvert. But you and I know the hobos around here keep to themselves and don't bother anyone. The killer didn't take Kent's money, so robbery wasn't a motive."

"Money? What money?"

"The bundle of cash his parents said he had."

Noelle did a double take. "How did you find them?"

"His missing persons report was filed in Riverbend, so I called every Calvert in the city until I found his folks. The parents told me their son wanted to leave home. They wouldn't give him the money. They told him to pay his own way. Then one day Kent showed up with a slew of cash. They were surprised because he didn't have a job. He said he didn't steal it, but he never said how he got it."

The money must have been a payment from the SIAMESE agent to deliver the filmstrip. "Okay, I admit I looked in Kent's wallet to find some identification and he had a gob of money. But I don't how where it came from." Noelle continued to chew on her sandwich.

"I think it was dirty money."

She stopped eating and played innocent. "Oh?"

"I'm thinking the cash might be a payoff for something crooked, like smuggling drugs. Why else would a man who had the cash for a bus ticket or rental car be walking around at night in the rain?"

She shrugged. "People do strange thing sometimes. Maybe he just liked taking long walks."

"I doubt that. I called my police contacts again to see if Calvert was a wanted criminal or an undercover cop. One of my sources got in touch with someone he knew in the FBI. They told him about some odd goings on in this area."

A lump grew in Noelle's throat. "Odd as in what?"

"He couldn't put a finger on it exactly. People popping up and disappearing. Large sums of cash moving around without leaving paper trails. The FBI contact said he's been talking to the CIA, and they report that Russian spies and secret data they've been tracking for months have been vanishing without their involvement. They think another spy group is working out there, but they can't locate them."

Was Trevor talking about SIAMESE or the "wild card" that ordered Bulldog's death? The best thing was for Noelle to get Trevor off this trail. If he started digging, he wouldn't stop until he had the street address of SIAMESE headquarters and Hanover's direct phone number.

"I think this all sounds silly. A kid from Riverbend wouldn't get mixed up with a sinister spy ring. That kind of stuff just doesn't happen around there. Looking for mysterious guys in trench coats is not going to help us find Kent Calvert's killer."

Trevor dipped a fry in a puddle of ketchup on his plate and munched it in silence. "Maybe you're right. I'll put this on the back burner. For now. Meanwhile, do you know who might have a motive to bump off Calvert?"

"Is this off the record? I don't want you printing accusations about innocent people."

"I'd never do that. But it might give me some leads to investigate."

Noelle shared what she knew about Gus E. Monty and May's friend. Then Trevor mentioned a man named Ted Markle.

"I know the name," she said. "He went to school here for a while. I never found out what happened to him."

"I did. Back in elementary school Kent humiliated Ted on a regular basis. Name calling, wedgies, insults, flushies, stealing his bag lunches, the works. Got so bad that the Markle family moved out of Yuletide just to avoid Kent. Ted wasn't happy to go, because he was a big star on the high school basketball team. He left behind a girlfriend as well. Ted was very fond of her. I know Ted pretty well. We've kept in touch over the years. When I told him about Kent's death he said, quote, 'Good for him! I wished I'd been there to fire the gun.'"

"But he has an alibi for that night, right?"

"Ted said he went to see a movie in Riverbend. He was alone, so nobody can corroborate his story. I talked to the theater staff. Despite the storm, the staff had a busy night. If Ted was there, he doesn't stand out in their minds. He has a strong motive and a flimsy alibi."

Chapter 19: Tell Me That Isn't True

"So many suspects, so little evidence." Noelle made a big deal of looking at her watch. "Is that the time? I need to go. I have an appointment. Thanks for the lunch." She scooted her chair back and stood up.

Trevor rose as well. "I'll be in touch. If you learn anything more about Calvert, you will let me know. Right?"

"Right."

"Let me walk you to your car."

"No, thanks, I really must run."

Actually she had plenty of time to meet with the Colonel, but she was tired of evading the reporter's questions. Trevor was one of her few close friends, the only man her age in this town she could tolerate, and she hated to give him the runaround. Was he going to keep probing into SIAMESE? What if he found out about her adventure of last night? Would he write it up for everyone in town to see? She better wrap up the murder case before he uncovered too much.

Noelle drove her Beetle downtown to the public library, where, as a kid, she had spent many happy hours tucked away amid the dimly-lit stacks, browsing in the various niches and side rooms stuffed with hardcover books. She parked the Bug and ran up the flight of concrete steps that led to the main entrance of the brick building. She pulled open the glass door and strolled into the quiet area of periodicals, newspapers and adult books (the kids' books were shelved downstairs). She greeted the librarians, who all knew her by name, and headed toward the Binhack Room, named for the town's first librarian. The women's reading circles used the space in the afternoons; teen study groups met there in the evenings.

Noelle entered the small room and closed the door behind her. "Hello, Colonel."

Harold Sieberson raised his head from the library books neatly laid out across the table before him and briskly rose to his feet to stand at attention. "Good afternoon, Miss McNabb." He gestured at one of the straight-back wooden chairs across the table. "At ease."

She took the offered chair. "What are you reading?"

Sieberson resumed his seat and waved at the old hardback tomes on the table. "I'm preparing a speech about the Normandy invasion for the VFW. Quite exciting. Here, take some of these." He gave her a handful of tri-fold brochures.

"What's this?" She scanned the full-color, professionally printed material.

"A pamphlet every good citizen should read and heed. It lists the ways we can keep our great country safe from the enemy forces that strive to destroy us. How we can watch for infiltration by the Communists."

"Really, Colonel, you don't believe the commies are around here, do you?"

He leaned over the table and spoke in hushed tones. "They're everywhere, no doubt listening to our every word." He straightened up and resumed a normal speaking voice. "Give those brochures to your friends. It's your patriotic duty."

"Thanks, Colonel." She absently stuffed the papers into her purse and set it on the floor. "You wanted to see me?"

"Yes, indeed." He pushed the books to one side and rested his forearms on the table. "At your request, I spoke with my contacts in Army intelligence regarding

SIAMESE. The organization originated within the CIA and for some time operated under its auspices. However, a new controller took over. That's when SIAMESE went rogue. This person felt hindered by CIA protocols. He wanted the freedom to operate in a different manner. The CIA felt the group was too reckless and foolhardy, resulting in a high fatality rate among its agents. The CIA has since tried to bring SIAMESE back under its wing, but like a feral cat, the group roams wherever it pleases. The CIA fears that the group will do something rash that will embarrass the government and possibly endanger authentic American agents."

"I see. Can't the government step in and remove the controller?"

"Attempts have been made, but like its namesake, SIAMESE slinks away and hides. Nobody can find them. Once they get a fix on this Hanover guy, he disappears."

The hair bristled on the back of her neck. "Hanover?"

"The SIAMESE controller. Dash Hanover."

Hiding her astonishment was the best piece of acting Noelle had ever done. So Dash was the person in charge of the whole shebang! He called the shots all along.

The colonel cocked his head. "Miss McNabb, are you all right?"

The question jolted her out of her thoughts. "Sorry, my mind wandered. What else did you find out?"

"Very little, except that the group seems to be active locally. The CIA has sent some men into the area to locate the renegades and shut down the operation."

Could the "wild card" involved in Bulldog's killing be a CIA agent? Was SIAMESE really acting in the best interests of the nation? Noelle's head spun. "Do you think that's a good idea? Shutting down SIAMESE, I mean. The group might actually be doing some good."

"I have heard no reports to support that thesis. Miss McNabb, if a SIAMESE agent approaches you, I strongly recommend that you tell me. I will immediately relay the information to the proper authorities."

"Oh, yes, yes, of course." With the poker face she struggled to maintain, Noelle could have played a high stakes table in Las Vegas. She picked up her purse. "I appreciate the information. If that's all, I should be going—"

"One more thing. I heard about the unfortunate murder of a young man last week. What was his name?"

"Kent Calvert."

"Yes. I suspect his death may be gang related."

"I don't think he was in a gang."

"What I mean to say is that a gang attacked him. The more unsavory criminal element in Riverbend has been attempting to establish a beachhead in Yuletide. They've been making overtures to the local gang of hoodlums."

"You mean Vince and his losers? No gang would want them. They're brainless blowhards. Give Vince a gun and he'd shoot off his own foot."

"Nevertheless, this death has the earmarks of a gang initiation. The ruffians discovered a man alone on a country road and harassed him. Perhaps the weapon fired accidentally, perhaps not, but when it did, the scoundrels retreated."

The last time Noelle had seen Vince, he had been sporting a wad of cash. Did one of the Riverbend gangs take him along on a crime spree? Did Vince take some of Kent's money? The local bad boy was dumb enough to ride along with a gang and do anything for someone's approval.

She asked, "Have you talked to Chief Whitlock about your theory?"

"Indeed I have. He shouldn't have much difficulty placing one of the gangs at the scene of the crime. On weekends they tear up and down the highways on their motorcycles. So I think we can all relax and not worry about a murderer in our town. After all, Noelle, you've lived here your whole life. Can you honestly picture any of our fine citizens as a killer?"

"I suppose not. That's a big relief off my mind. Thanks, Colonel."

"You're welcome. Dismissed."

She wasn't completely satisfied with his deduction, but Sieberson opened one of the books and bent his head down to read, indicating the discussion was over. Soon she was back at the cottage, stepping over Ceebee as he danced around her ankles. She gave him some cat treats as the phone rang. When she answered, Destiny gave her a report of her visit to the Hildebrand family. She'd met with Otto's next of kin, a brother and daughter-in-law. Posing as a journalist, Destiny quizzed them, but came up empty-handed. The brother insisted that Otto had no dealing with spies, criminals or Russians. In fact, the deceased had been in a coma during his final days. Otto also had no friends, relatives or business associates who might be involved in espionage. When the spy prodded further, the man ordered Density out of the home.

"Do you believe him?" Noelle asked.

"I can sense when someone's trying to fool me, but these folks were straight up. As for having the microdot, Hildebrand is a wash-up."

"What about the obituary itself? Was it written in code?"

"We ran it past our code experts and checked the

paper for watermarks or hidden ink. Nothing."

"Thanks for letting me know. I thought Hanover had kicked me off the case."

"Technically, yes, but I knew you wanted know."

Destiny hung up without so much as a goodbye. Noelle was getting used to the curt behavior of SIAMESE agents. She wanted to ask the spy if the Colonel's accusations about the organization were true, but if they were, Destiny would only deny them. Noelle popped open a bottle of Frostie and sank in the sofa. She sipped the soft drink as Ceebee kneaded her lap. Murder, Russians and suspects swirled about in her mind. She needed to chill out and take her mind off the spy-versus-spy craziness. Noelle picked up the *TV Guide* from the coffee table and flipped the pages. Maybe she could find a harmless, silly sitcom to distract her from reality. Plenty of fluffy TV choices on a Thursday night: *Batman, F Troop, My Three Sons, Bewitched* and *That Girl*. Good thing she wasn't at her parents' house. Her kid brother would confiscate the TV at seven-thirty for *Star Trek*. Which reminded her, only two more days until her favorite show returned. Maybe this time she could watch it uninterrupted.

A thought popped into her mind. Noelle dropped the *TV Guide* and picked up the phone. She left an urgent message at the SIAMESE switchboard for Destiny to call her immediately.

A few minutes later she got a call back "What's up?"

"Listen, Destiny. I know where the microdot is hidden."

Chapter 19: Tombstone Blues

"You're crazy, girl. We tried everything," said Destiny.

"Not everything. The obituary clue isn't about a person—it's a place. Listen. In one episode of *Mission: Impossible,* the IM Force is trying to find some Nazi gold. They go to a cemetery, and the gold is hidden inside the walls of a crypt. I think the microdot is stashed somewhere around Hildebrand's grave. Why else would Bulldog carry around that obit?"

"Noelle, that's the smartest thing I've heard you say. Let me run that by Hanover. If he's cool with that, I'll check it out."

"Aren't we going together?"

"The boss wants you to lay low."

"Please, Destiny. This is my idea, and two people can search faster than one. I'm in this thing knee deep all ready, so what's the harm?"

"You're in only if Dash gives the high sign."

Apparently Hanover approved, because a short time later Destiny arrived at the cottage. As always, she looked classy even in a tight black jumpsuit and black ankle boots. A small black pouch hung from her gun belt. This time her weapon was in plain sight, in a holster. She told Noelle to put on black clothes and bring a flashlight if she had one. Noelle changed into the outfit she wore when she worked backstage crew on a play: black slacks, black long-sleeved turtleneck shirt and black socks and sneakers. From a hall closet Noelle dug out her rectangular metal "hunter" flashlight with a huge lens and a handle across the top. She'd often used the light on her Girl Scout camping trips.

Destiny glanced at her partner. "Don't you have a flashlight that's smaller than a lighthouse?"

"This is all I have, sorry."

After a quick drive, they were stepping over flower vases and dodging headstones at the Eternal Peace Memorial Cemetery near the Riverbend city limits. Clouds obscured the moon, casting long shadows over the ground. The damp, grassy earth muffled their footsteps. The only sounds were the wind in the trees and the low buzz of cicadas. The cool night air cut through the black jacket Noelle had zipped over her clothes. Or maybe her chills came from being in a graveyard after dark. Eventually they found Otto Hildebrand's headstone, a four-foot-high marker made of red marble. A floral arrangement from the recent funeral service decorated the front of the memorial.

Destiny ran her detection cube over the ground and the flowers. "Nothing."

"Maybe it's in the coffin," said Noelle.

Even in the darkness Noelle could see her partner's eyes flash. "Now what's the point of hiding something in a sealed-up coffin stuck six feet underground? We don't have time to dig up dead folk."

Noelle frowned. "Just a thought." She inadvertently took a step back and fell over the headstone.

Destiny grabbed Noelle's hand and pulled her to her feet. "Watch it!"

The spy stared at the marker for a minute and ran her hand over the letters cut deep into the rock. She ran the device over the engraved name. The cube glowed red and beeped. Destiny stuck her fingers inside the cut letters. From deep inside the letter "a," she removed a white capsule and shone her penlight beam on it.

"There's our beauty!" she said.

"Kinda big for a microdot, isn't it?"

"The dot's inside the capsule."

Behind a clump of trees a car drove up. The motor shut off.

Destiny stuck the capsule into the pouch hanging from her belt. "Let's get out of here."

They retraced their steps through the grounds, past the stone benches and angel statues.

Destiny held up a hand to stop Noelle. "Shhh. I hear someone."

The crunch of footsteps on dried leaves sounded close—too close. They turned and stared straight into the beam of a flashlight. Noelle held up a hand to block the glare.

A man dressed in dark clothes held the flashlight in one hand and a gun in the other. By his voice the women could tell he was black. His speech was low but urgent. "Hand over the microdot."

Destiny instinctively raised her hands shoulder-height. "Whatcha talking about, bro?"

"Don't jive me. I saw you take it from that grave."

He raised the gun. Noelle gasped. She'd played with prop pistols in her stage combat class in college, but this piece of hardware didn't shoot blanks. Her eagerness to work with the spies had landed her in one not-so-fine mess.

Destiny stayed calm. "Who you working for? The KGB ain't got Negroes."

"Don't mess with me, girl. Five seconds or you'll be just like these corpses."

Noelle's eyes darted between Destiny and the man. She held her breath.

Destiny sneezed, loud and hard. "This night air messes up my sinuses." She reached for her pouch. The man's finger tightened on the trigger.

"Don't shoot!" Noelle yelled.

The man turned the gun on her.

"Hush, child!" Destiny told her. To the man she said, "Chill, bro. I gotta get a hanky so I don't get snot down my threads." With two fingers and thumb she pulled a Kleenex from her bag and blew her nose. "Hang tight. I'll get you the goods." She crammed the tissue back in her pouch, removed a white capsule, and held out her arm. "The microdot's inside."

The man tucked the flashlight under an arm, grabbed the capsule, and ran away.

"Let's get him!" Noelle said.

Destiny grabbed her arm. "That's what he wants us to do. His goons may be waiting to ambush us."

"But we can't let him get away with—"

"Come on!"

Destiny jerked her arm. Noelle obediently followed. The women didn't speak until they were in the car, roaring down the highway.

"I'm sorry I screwed things up," said Noelle.

"Screwed what up?"

"If I hadn't told you about the cemetery, the bad guy wouldn't have the microdot."

"Who said he did?" With one hand on the steering wheel, Destiny reached into her pouch with the other and extracted a white capsule.

"But I saw you give the guy—"

"—a cold tablet. I always carry one. I can't afford to get sick."

Noelle laughed. "Destiny, you're the best."

The driver opened a tiny panel in the dashboard and dropped the capsule inside the compartment. "I had to do something since you didn't jump the guy."

"But he had a gun."

"He didn't have eyes in the back of his head. It was dark. He didn't see you until you blabbed. You could have sneaked up from behind and punched and kicked.

I could have grabbed his weapon. If you're going to tag along, you gotta be more useful."

Noelle stared out the side window. "Sorry. I really want to help."

"Tell you what. I'm headed for HQ. Company rules, all classified data must be turned in PDQ. While we're there, I'll ask the self-defense coach to teach you some moves."

Noelle looked at Destiny and brightened. "That sounds great. Thanks."

Not only did Noelle like the idea of proving herself, but the possibility of finding the location of SIAMESE headquarters also pleased her. The car had clear glass windows, so she could easily follow the route. However, as they sped along the highway, the gentle rocking of the car lulled her to sleep. She didn't open her eyes again until Destiny had parked the car in the SIAMESE underground garage. When Noelle finished her self-defense training, another agent drove her home in a vehicle with tinted windows. If she was going to participate in dangerous missions, why didn't the spies trust her with their office address?

Chapter 20: I've Gotta Get A Message To You Friday

Dressed in grubby, knock-around-the-house clothes, Noelle was enjoying a late breakfast of oatmeal and fruit when her mother called.

"Hi, sweetie, where have you been? I've been calling for two days and you never answered."

Noelle gulped as she sank onto the sofa. She usually touched base with Mom a few times a week, but she'd been too preoccupied with spy capers to call. Mom was bound to get suspicious when she hadn't checked in.

"I've been busy, Mom."

"You said you were doing some acting in Riverbend. Is that where you've been?"

"Yeah, that's right." Unlike Trevor, at least Mom hadn't snooped around the ad agencies.

"Have you been out of town overnight?"

"Are you checking up on me?"

"Of course not. But Riverbend can be a dangerous place at night for a single girl."

If Mom knew that her daughter was poking around dead bodies in dark alleys and tramping through cemeteries at night, she'd worry herself sick.

"I'm all right, Mom, really. I can take care of myself."

"So what is this acting job? You always like to tell me about the plays you're in. Is it something your father and I can see?"

Noelle took as deep breath. She just couldn't spew out a string of lies to her mother. Sooner or later someone was bound to discover the truth and she'd be forced to concoct even more fibs. Unlike Destiny and Dash, she couldn't live behind a façade. She'd have to eventually tell Mom about her involvement with SIAMESE. But what about her promise to Dash? What if he was listening in on her call?

"Well, Mom, it isn't exactly acting. I mean, in a way it is but . . . You remember when I was a kid you told me the importance of keeping a secret? What I'm doing now is a secret."

"Are you in some kind of trouble?"

"No, no, nothing like that."

"You're not making dirty movies, are you?"

"Mother! Of course not! What if I told you I was doing something for the good of the country?"

"Noelle, you're not making any sense."

Even if she could talk about her spy work, Mom wouldn't approve of her dancing like a maniac inside a smoky nightclub or standing at the business end of a handgun.

"It's a very special project, and the producers want to keep it quiet until it's finished. You know how it is. They're afraid word will get out and their competitors will beat them to the punch with a similar project."

"Oh, I see. I think."

"Look, it'll all be over soon. I'll be working at the park this weekend. And believe me, Mom, I'm all right. Nobody's holding a gun to my head." Someone had threatened her last night, but not at this moment.

"You know you can always talk to me about anything. I'm always here to listen."

"I know, Mom, and I appreciate that."

"If you're involved in something important, I'd like to share it with the other ladies. They're always bragging about their kids starting families."

Noelle sighed. Her mother felt left out when her lady

friends boasted about their grandkids. She longed to tell Mom that the work she was doing was keeping the world safe for these kids.

"Sure, Mom. And I'm having a good time. Really."

"Stay safe. Love you."

"Love you too, Mom. Wait, before you go, I have a question. Do I have an aunt named Grizelda?"

A pause. "Who?"

"Grizelda."

"That name doesn't sound familiar."

Her own mother just lied to her! Noelle couldn't believe it. "Don't you have a sister named Grizelda?"

"You must mean Cynthia. I can't keep up with her name changes. She's been through a couple of marriages." Now her mother sounded suspicious. "How did you hear about her?"

"Someone told me."

"This is something we need to talk about in person. Maybe sometime when you come over to the house." With that Mom gave a quick goodbye and hung up.

Noelle replaced the phone receiver with a strange aching feeling. She really wanted to share the most exciting thing that had ever happened to her. Surely Hanover wouldn't mind if she told just one person. Did he ever talk to his mother about his work? And speaking of Hanover's parents, her own mother wasn't interested in discussing her sister, as indicated by the vague "sometime." Just who was this mystery woman?

But for now Noelle had other matters to tend to—such as laundry. She carried a wicker basket of dirty clothes to the landlords' house. The couple allowed Noelle the use of the washer and dryer at the main house so she wouldn't have to drive into town to the Laundromat. Noelle had a key to the back door that opened directly into the laundry room. She started a load of colors and returned to the cottage in time to catch another phone call.

As always, Hanover didn't waste time but lunged straight to the point. "We need a fresh face for a message drop."

"A what for a what?"

"One of our contacts is sending us information regarding the final microdot. Our regular agents are too well known, so we need someone new that the enemy doesn't recognize."

"Like me."

"Yes, like you."

"Will Destiny be with me?"

"No, she's on another assignment. Besides, having two people on a message drop is too conspicuous. And Miss King is, shall we say, likely to attract attention."

"'Cause she's prettier than I am."

"I did not say that."

"Will this be dangerous?"

"Not if you follow instructions."

"Okay, shoot. I mean, go ahead."

The mission was set at the Raintree Mall in Riverbend—already this sounded like fun. Noelle loved shopping at the big, modern shopping center that was far superior to Yuletide's mom-and-pop shops with their limited merchandise, crowded aisles and décor that hadn't been updated since the 1950s. The scheme was this: at the mall, Noelle would take her time browsing instead of going directly to the encounter site to detour any tails. Her goal was the Orange Julius stand.

"Orange Julius!" she exclaimed. "That's my favorite drink!"

"Make sure no other customers are in earshot. Order a pineapple extra frothy and extra large."

"But Orange Julius doesn't have a pineapple flavor or an extra large size."

"I know. That's the password. The clerk will hand you a special cup. Take the cup inside the ladies' room. If you're followed, that will put off the tail."

"What if a woman is following me?"

"Go immediately go into a stall and lock it. The enemy won't kick down a restroom door. But work quickly. Once you're inside the stall, dump the drink down the toilet."

"Why can't I drink it? Will it be poisoned?"

Even though Noelle couldn't see Hanover, somehow she sensed he was irritated. "Your goal is to retrieve the information, not indulge your thirst. The message will be written on the inside bottom of the cup. Once the message is exposed to air, the letters will only be visible for thirty seconds. You must memorize the message in that time. Do not write it down. The enemy can easily steal a slip of paper. Once the message is fully dissolved, place the cup in the trash bin and go to the enclosed phone booths in the north side of the mall. Call HQ and relay the message. I'll give you a special phone number to use that will scramble your message to any phone taps. But the number can only be used once, so get the message correct on your first call. Then go home."

"That's all I have to do?"

"That's all you have to do."

"Can I stay at the mall afterwards and shop?"

His normally evenhanded veneer began to crack. "Will you please stay focused on the mission?" He made her repeat the instructions and the special phone number three times to make sure she had it down pat.

"Now I have a question for you," Noelle said. "Last night, Destiny thought the man who held us up wasn't a Russian."

"Yes, she informed me of that fact during the debriefing. Miss King described the man to us, but we have no record of him in our files. Either he's a newcomer to the business, or he's operating with invisibility."

"Do you think he's working with the guy I saw at the nightclub?"

"That we don't know."

"And about that guy at the table. Did you find out about him?"

"Yes, he's a hired assassin. We've encountered him before. His M.O. is to pick up a companion so he can blend in with the people around him. A lone guy sitting in a nightclub is too obvious. What we don't know is who hired him to eliminate Bulldog. Could be the Russians, the man at the graveyard or somebody else."

"Just how many spies are there out in the world?"

"If we knew that, they wouldn't be doing their job. So be careful, Miss McNabb. Other parties are desperate to retrieve the microdot. If someone is tailing you at the mall, leave immediately. We'll arrange an alternate plan. If someone intercepts you after you've made pickup, hand over the cup. Don't fight and don't be a hero. You will be of no use to us dead."

"I'll remember that."

She hung up and went to the bedroom to change clothes. For the mission she might need to run, so she put on blue slacks, a matching blue plaid long-sleeved shirt, socks, brown loafers and a windbreaker.

The opening of Raintree Mall was yet another blow that led to the demise of Riverbend's downtown. The building's contemporary design appealed to youth. The covered interior provided shelter from bad weather, encouraging guests to stay a long time. Shoppers could eat, visit a variety of shops, and even watch a movie without driving from store to store or paying a parking meter. At the time of construction, the west end of the city consisted of fields for grazing dairy cows, a wide open space that was perfect for the sprawling, two-story complex and ample free off-street parking. The city had grown around the mall, enclosing it with blocks of single-family homes and smaller shopping areas offering grocery stories and services.

Inside the mall, Noelle soaked up the experience. Huge mobiles made of metal rods hung from the translucent ceiling. Piped-in light pop music created a carnival atmosphere. Water gurgled from a fountain in the middle of the open floor. Even at mid-day, busy shoppers hurried through the space. Noelle wandered by the endless stores lining the exterior walls. She passed Montgomery Wards, Woolworth's, a record store (larger than Groovy Vinyl and one that handled imports) and a jewelry shop. She resisted the urge to duck into the fashion store to check out the new Mary Quant minis and blouses that graced the manikins in the window.

At the Orange Julius kiosk she waited behind another customer. After he left, she smiled at the clerk, a middle-age woman who didn't look like a spy—but neither did Noelle.

"If I said I wanted a pineapple extra frothy, would you know what that meant?"

"Yes, ma'am." The clerk greeted her as she would any customer, with no special recognition or surprise. "Small, medium or large?"

"Extra large."

The clerk picked up a cup from behind the counter—it looked like the standard large size—and opened a spigot to fill the cup with the yummy orange liquid. Noelle preferred the strawberry drink, but asking the clerk to change the flavor might mess up the mission. When the cup had filled, the clerk snapped a plastic lid on the cup, set it on the counter and asked for money.

"What for?" Noelle asked.

"That's the cost of the drink."

"I have to pay to pick up the message?"

"You have to pay for the drink." The clerk kept her hand on the cup.

Noelle dug out her coin purse and handed over some coins. Not a high price, but maybe SIAMESE would reimburse her for the cost. The clerk handed back the change. Noelle took the cup as well as a straw from the dispenser. She let her purse hang from her arm and jabbed the straw through the slit in the lid and sipped. Regardless of Hanover's instructions, she was going to drink the ambrosia. She'd never dump such deliciousness down the drain. Now that she had the message, was someone following her? Noelle had been so busy window shopping she'd forgotten to check for tails. She dodged a young mother pushing a stroller. She stood by one of the supporting pillars, trying to look like an ordinary shopper. She eyed the other customers. How would she know if someone was after her? Noelle roamed the floor while sipping the drink, glancing back to see if anyone was sticking to her. She saw nothing unusual, but perhaps the tail was good at hiding. To shake off any potential enemies, she rode to the escalator to the second floor, walked the balcony that circled the building, returned to ground level and ducked into the women's restroom.

One lady was washing her hands, and another was fixing her makeup at a mirror. Both of them ignored Noelle. The wanna-be spy locked herself into a stall. She ripped off the lid and gulped down the rest of the drink. She inspected the bottom of the cup. Nothing. Had the clerk given her the wrong cup? Then letters appeared on the cup bottom; apparently the ink needed time to activate. With her actor's training, Noelle quickly memorized the words.

'Black stallion leaps high. Round and round. Red

jewel. Saddle up.'
   What on earth did that mean?

Chapter 21: On a Carousel

The letters on the paper cup faded away. Noelle flushed the toilet so any snoopers would think she'd actually used it, then left the stall. She dropped the crumbled cup into the trash bin and washed her hands. She was hungry. Hanover wanted her to call right away, but he'd have to wait a few minutes while she had lunch. One worked up an appetite in the service of her country, and besides, the crazy message didn't seem urgent. At the first-floor food court she ordered a cheeseburger and fries. Sitting at a molded plastic table, she ruminated as she ate. Was the message in code? Did 'black horse' mean a certain building or street? Was it a reference to a stable? Plenty of people in the outlying rural areas rode horses, and many owned black horses. Go round and round a racetrack? Did 'red jewel' refer to a horse decorated for a parade? But the next big parade in the area was on Fourth of July, months away. Could 'leaps high' be a horse in a steeplechase? But how could anyone remove a microdot from a jumping animal?

A mother and a fidgety child took a nearby table. As the mom doled out the sandwiches and drinks, the boy said. "Mommy, I wanna go to the zoo!"

"We're in town to see the dentist. If we have time, we'll go to the zoo after your teeth are cleaned. Now hurry and eat so you'll have time to brush you teeth."

"Why do I gots to brush my teeth if the dentist is gonna clean them?"

"Hush now and eat."

"I don't wanna see the dentist. I wanna go to the zoo and ride the horsies."

The amusement park inside the county zoo—of course! Noelle had been there many times as a kid herself. 'Round and round' must be the zoo carousel. The data must be hidden on a black merry-go-round horse. That made more sense than trying to pick a microdot off a stubborn live animal. She couldn't wait to tell Dash she'd figured out the clue. Then he'd realize she had brains after all. Better yet, she'd fetch the microdot herself. Why not? The zoo was only a short drive from the mall. She'd grab the object and return home in less time than it would take for an agent to arrive. Hanover would be pleased with her. Noelle wolfed down her food, returned the plastic tray to the tray station and hurried to her car.

School was still in session, so the park only had a few visitors, just some older couples and moms with infants. At the merry-go-round Noelle paid the attendant (another charge for SIAMESE to reimburse), circled the rows of plastic animals and found the one black horse. She climbed aboard the animal just as the pre-recorded calliope music started and the floor began to turn. Instead of watching the scenery fly by, she bent over to inspect the colorful stones glued on the horse. With one hand she clutched the silver pole that bisected the horse, and the other she ran along the thick neck. Noelle shifted in the seat for balance as the horse rose and fell to the organ music. The message said 'red stone,' so the microdot must be inside a scarlet gem— but which one? If she had Destiny's little cube detector, her job would be easier. And what did 'saddle up' mean? Was the red stone in or under the saddle? She touched all the decorations on the horse's neck and head, but no hidden doors sprang open. An inspection of the horse's flank yielded nothing.

"Mommy, what is that lady doing?"

Noelle raised her head. Two rows to her left, a child was riding a camel. The tot's mother stood on the floor and held her. Both of them stared at her. Noelle blushed. In her eagerness she'd forgotten she was sneaking around in broad daylight.

"I'm just admiring the fine artwork on the horse," she said.

Apparently that satisfied the family as they turned their attention to the other riders. The merry-go-round music slowed and so did the ride. Over so soon? Noelle had found nothing, and she refused to fork over more money for another turn. The attendant walked by, ordering the riders to leave. Noelle dismounted and hooked her purse strap over an elbow, but didn't step away. On the side of the saddle she spied a huge red stone. The attendant was occupied with the young passengers, so he didn't see Noelle crouch behind the horse, out of view of those standing on the ground. She touched the red stone. It seemed a little loose. She wiggled it, but it didn't fall off the animal. From her purse she removed a metal rattail comb and dug the pointed end of the handle beneath the rock. If she could pry it out before the next ride started, she'd be home free. The empty spot wouldn't be noticeable, at least not with someone in the saddle. She forced the comb under the stone, and the rock popped out.

"What do you think you're doing, miss?"

Noelle looked up into a pair of silver sunglasses that reflected her face back to her. The man wore the gray uniform of a zoo security guard.

"Nothing." She straightened up and crammed the comb and the stone into her purse, hoping the guard hadn't see the purloined item.

"Come with me, please."

"But I want to ride another turn."

"I saw you destroy city property."

"I didn't tear up anything. I just noticed that some of these stones are loose."

He didn't move or smile. Noelle followed him across the park as the passers-by stared at them. They entered a one-story, nondescript administration building. He took her to a small, sparsely furnished office. Behind a desk sat a woman wearing a neat suit and glasses and with her hair in a bun. The plastic zoo badge on her left breast identified her as the director of zoo operations. She didn't look pleased to see Noelle.

"I saw this girl vandalizing one of the carousel horses," said the guard.

"No, I wasn't, ma'am," Noelle responded. "I was taking a close look at it. I thought I saw some scratches that someone else had made. From where the guard was standing, maybe it looked like I was doing something, but I wasn't."

"Our officers have very good vision," said the woman. "What is your name?"

Noelle considering giving a fake name, but if they looked at her driver's license, they'd know she was lying. So she told them the truth.

The woman said, "I won't press charges if you leave the property immediately."

"But I did nothing wrong!"

"Do I need to call the police?"

Noelle was furious, but the cops might make things worse and even arrest her. So she complied. As she and the guard left the office, the director scribbled a note on a clipboard, no doubt adding her name to a list of troublemakers. Noelle McNabb had never been in trouble with the law before, not even for a ticket at an expired parking meter. Now she had a criminal record. At the zoo exit gate the guard dismissed her with a cheerless "have a nice day." What gall! She shot him the meanest look she could muster and stomped away.

At least she escaped with the stone. Noelle could turn over the microdot to Hanover and still be a hero. Back home she sat at the kitchen table and examined every inch of the red plastic blob. She didn't see or feel any bumps, no cracks or seams that would open and reveal a hiding place. Maybe the microdot was embedded inside? She took the pink-handled hammer from her handywoman's tool kit and lightly tapped the rock. The stone crumbled into pieces. A careful inspection of each bit of dust revealed nothing. But all the clues fit. The data must be here.

The phone rang. "Did you make the drop?" said Hanover. "I expected your call hours ago. Did something go wrong?"

"I found the rock. I mean, I got the rock that's suppose to have the microdot but I can't find it."

"What are you talking about?"

"I figured out what the secret message said. And I went to get the dot myself."

"McNabb!" His voice rose an octave. "Under no circumstances are you ever to go against orders! You were to let us handle the retrieval. Our agents can move in and out unnoticed. Did you run into any trouble?"

"No—not really."

"Explain."

She told him the message and what she did at the park, leaving out the part about the guard and getting booted off the grounds. She didn't lie, exactly, just omitted some of the truth. Fudging on the truth was getting easier to do. Was she losing her morals?

After a brief pause, Hanover replied. "And we still don't have the data."

"It must be inside this rock."

"If so, you would have seen it. Microdots are not invisible. It's possible you destroyed it with your hammering."

"But the message seemed to say—"

"That's why you let the professionals handle these situations. Our codes are always changing. 'Black horse' might not refer to an animal. You've wasted valuable time."

"I'm sorry. I just wanted to help."

"The way to help us is to follow instructions precisely. No more, no less."

"Give me another chance. I'll do better next time."

"You are not longer of any use to SIAMESE." He hung up.

The words cut her worse than any audition rejection. For ten minutes she cried. What did she do wrong? Nobody had been hurt or killed. She had revealed no secrets. She'd worked hard and tried her best but still failed. What did Hanover know, the heartless beast? To him she was no better than the tissues she was using to wipe her eyes. He didn't care who got hurt while he played his stupid spy games.

She glanced at the Felix wall clock. Not only had she been booted out of SIAMESE, but she was also late for her job at the park. Noelle had missed the Friday walkthrough, a quick rehearsal to refresh everyone after a week off. She could still make the performance if she rushed. Or she could call in sick and let the understudy take over. No, she'd only sit at home all evening and cry some more. Acting would at least take her mind off her woes and maybe the applause would cheer her up.

With no time to change clothes, Noelle hastily poured a bowl of kibble for Ceebee, grabbed her purse and jacket, and dashed outside to the garage. She sped through town in the Bug, with one eye out to make sure the cops didn't catch her speeding. At the park she ran toward the theater, dodging the clumps of dawdling tourists. She raced through the Childhood Playground of kiddie rides. Then she stopped dead in her tracks.

Ahead of her stood the majestic carousel with its rows of colorful lights and wooden hand-carved animals. On the outer row rose a gallant black stallion, covered in bright jewels, with its front hooves kicking high in the air.

Chapter 22: You Know My Name (Look Up The Number)

Of course! The secret message had to mean the merry-go-round at the Country Christmas park. A spy could easily travel to Yuletide and the enemy, like her, would assume the spy had placed the microdot somewhere in Riverbend. Anyone could easily come through the entry gate after paying admission. The gate attendants didn't keep track of the guests' names or addresses. The hosts and hostesses—as the employees who worked with the public were called—would pay more attention to the enthusiastic children than to a single adult quietly minding his business. Nobody would notice a spy sliding a microdot onto a carousel horse.

Noelle bit her lip. As much as she wanted to call Hanover immediately, her job took priority. She put on her costume and makeup in record time with seconds to spare before her entrance. Noelle rushed her lines, eager to get off stage to talk to SIAMESE. After the curtain call, Noelle was the first one to rush down the backstage steps. She stopped by the pay phone in the hall outside the dressing rooms and dropped a dime into the phone slot, hoping SIAMESE was a local call. She faced the wall, cupped her hand over the mouthpiece, and spoke softly so the other cast members wouldn't hear.

"This is Tabby Gray. I need to speak with Fido Brown right now. I know he's there."

The operator spoke in her usual unemotional voice.

"Ma'am, you're calling on an unsecured line."

"I can't get to my phone until later. This is urgent."

"Fido Brown cannot take calls over an unsecured line."

"He'll take this one if he wants the microdot."

A pause. "One moment, please."

Noelle tapped her finger on the wall phone as she waited, hoping she wouldn't have to drop more money into the slot. Some elves passed by, and she smiled at them. Then one of the seven-year-old snowflakes in the show tugged on her skirt.

"I have to call my mom," the kid said.

"Sure, as soon as I finish my call."

"But you're not talking to nobody."

"I'm on hold."

"I need mommy to come and pick me up RIGHT NOW."

"Can't you wait a minute? This is important."

"I have to get home so I can—"

A familiar voice came over the earpiece. "Fido Brown. Why are you calling over an open line?"

Noelle turned her back to the snowflake. "I know where the microdot is."

"I can't afford to send out more agents on another wild goose chase. We inspected the merry-go-round at the zoo and found nothing."

"It was the wrong one! We've got a carousel here at the Christmas theme park in Yuletide. There's a big black dancing horse, just as the message says. This has to be the one."

"I'll check into it and see if we need to investigate."

"You need me on this one. I know the park layout and the schedule of the security guard."

Snowflake jabbed her finger into Noelle's leg. "Hurry up!"

Hanover said, "Who's that?"

"Nobody important," Noelle replied. "I get off work in a couple of hours. I can meet the agent at—"

Hanover cut in. "We're picking up a tracer on this line." He hung up.

Noelle replaced the receiver and walked away. The idea of the call being tapped unnerved her. Had she jeopardized the mission? Worse yet, did the enemy know where she worked? Was the hired assassin who'd killed Bulldog on his way to bump her off as well? She toyed with the idea of skipping out and letting the understudy take over the remaining shows tonight, but she wouldn't be any safer at home. Besides, the understudy played the witch as a crabby old woman with a tummy ache, and the tourists who traveled far to visit the park deserved better than that. As the night wore on, Noelle hung around the other actors as they gossiped backstage between the shows. She disliked their company, but she felt more secure in a crowd.

After the final show of the evening, she bolted down the stairs, changed clothes and raced to her car. To get home as fast as she could, Noelle put the pedal to the metal—that is, until a police car siren wailed and a red light flashed in her rearview mirror. Of all the times to get stopped by the cops! Noelle pulled over to the curb and fumed as Chief Whitlock waddled up to her door. She rolled down the window.

He leaned in and placed his hairy hands on the window ledge. "Goin' a little fast back there, aren't we, missy? What's the speed limit for this street?" His eyes bugged out. "What in tarnation happened to your face?"

"My face?"

"You're green as a lime. Are you sick?"

Noelle touched her cheek. She had been in such a hurry to leave the park that she'd forgotten to remove her witch's makeup. But she smiled. She just might get out of this ticket.

"Yes, that's it. I'm sick. I have a highly contagious skin disease. I have to get to a doctor for treatment before it spreads."

"Really?"

"Yeah, I don't feel so good." She gave an exaggerated cough.

Whitlock removed his hands from the auto. "You better go see that doctor right away. Do you need a police escort?"

"No, that won't be necessary, thanks."

He backed away. "Yeah, that's really ugly looking. Hope you get feeling better soon."

Noelle wait until the patrol car drove away before she burst out laughing. Maybe she should wear the green makeup any time she wanted to drive fast. Once she arrived home, she washed the green goo off her face and fed Ceebee, who went to sleep off the meal on the sofa. Noelle warmed up some leftover spaghetti and meatballs and green beans for her dinner. Should she phone Hanover or wait for him to return her call? After the way she'd bungled the mission earlier today, he might not want to speak to her at all. She switched on the radio. The local station had just started its broadcast of the Yuletide High home basketball game. For those who didn't go to the movies on Friday nights, the school games were the big entertainment. But listening to a disembodied voice full of static lacked the same zest as sitting in the bleachers with the crowd vibe and cheering on the Elves in person. She switched off the radio and flopped on the sofa. Maybe Hanover didn't trust her anymore. Couldn't he give her one more chance to redeem herself? She resigned herself to a lonely evening of living vicariously through the adventures of secret agents Napoleon Solo and Illya Kuryakin on NBC.

Someone knocked on the door. She wasn't in the

mood to deal with a tourist who'd gotten lost looking for a shortcut to the highway. "Go away!"

From the other side of the door came an equally irritated voice. "Do you want to find the microdot or not?"

"Destiny!" Noelle sprang to her feet and opened the door. "I wasn't expecting you."

"Who'd you think it was, the Jolly Green Giant?"

Noelle almost couldn't see Destiny standing in the doorway. In her black leather jumpsuit and black gun holster, the spy blended into the nighttime. A fine mesh scarf was tied around her neck.

"So Hanover said I could be on the assignment?" said Noelle.

"No. He did not authorize you. But I think you might be useful. I'm sticking my neck out for you, Noelle. If I don't return with the microdot, Dash will have my head on a platter. So don't mess up."

"I won't, I won't."

"So get dressed and let's go."

Noelle's heart jumped. She was working with Destiny again! She rushed to the bedroom and quickly threw on her black slacks and turtleneck outfit, dropping her other clothes in a heap on the floor. She grabbed her house key and the "hunter" lantern. When she returned to the living room, Destiny was holding and petting a purring Ceebee. Her face had a calm and peaceful look. And for the first time since Noelle had known her, Destiny was smiling.

"That's weird," said Noelle. "Ceebee usually doesn't take to strangers."

"Hmmm?" Destiny looked up and the smile dropped. A flicker of embarrassment crossed her face. She set the cat on the floor. Her all-business composure returned. "You ready?"

"I'm ready."

Destiny looked her over. "We gotta get you a better flashlight."

Chapter 23: It's a Gas

On the way to the park, Destiny overshot the speed limit and Noelle panicked, afraid that Whitlock would pull them over, but the cop was nowhere around. Maybe Noelle's "disease" had scared him off patrol for the rest of the night.

"How do we get in the park so nobody sees us?" Destiny asked.

"There's three entrances," said Noelle. "The main gate and—"

"We don't go waltzing in through a gate. Is there a wall or fence we can climb over?"

"There's a chain-link fence around the back."

"Groovy."

"But it's too wobbly to climb."

"We can cut through it. Where do I hide the car?"

"There's a one-lane dirt road that runs behind the park. It's mostly used by the delivery trucks. But the carousel is up front near the guest entrance. We'd have to walk all the way through the park."

"That's cool. Is the cleaning crew gone?"

"Yeah, they should be. They start working as soon as the park closes."

As they neared their destination, Destiny switched from the regular headlights to the infrared night beams. She could still see the road without the lights giving away their location. The car turned onto the service road and passed by a thick but neatly trimmed row of shrubbery on the right.

"The fence is on the other side of the hedge," Noelle

said. "This would be a good spot to sneak in, behind the restaurant."

Destiny parked the car behind some trees. The women got out. The spy popped the trunk and removed a set of grass clippers and a bolt cutter with long handles. They both squatted behind the hedge.

"What time does the guard pass by?" Destiny asked.

Noelle tilted her wrist to try and catch the moonlight on her watch. "I can't see the time."

"You need a luminous dial." Destiny pushed back her sleeve and revealed a watch face that glowed a bright green.

Noelle leaned over to see the dial. "That's pretty neat. Wait five minutes, and then the coast should be clear."

They crouched in silence. The tall grass tickled Noelle's ankles and her legs started to cramp. In the stillness, her breathing sounded like a hurricane. The crickets made a gentle hum. In the distance came the faint sounds of highway traffic. The minutes dragged like hours. Just as Noelle thought about stretching her arms she heard footsteps. Destiny put a finger to her lips. Noelle froze. On the other side of the hedge, hard-sole shoes slapped the concrete walkway and moved onto the ground. The grass crunched beneath the guard's shoes. A flashlight beam poked through the gaps in the hedge. The walker stopped. Could the guard see them through the greenery? Noelle held her breath. The back of her neck itched. She struggled not to scratch. Finally the steps moved away, growing softer in volume. Noelle let out a sigh of relief. Destiny waited a moment longer to make certain the guard had passed. She clipped a slot in the hedge for them to slide through. With the bolt cutters she snipped through the metal links of the fence.

Destiny whispered. "How much time before the next

guard round?"

"An hour. Plenty of time."

"Never assume that. Routines have a way of changing when you don't expect it. We need to move fast. In and out. And don't talk."

Destiny left the cutters on the ground, got on her belly, and wriggled through the hole in the fence. On the other side, she motioned for Noelle to follow. As the actress squirmed through the opening in the fence, the sharp cut edges of the wire poked at her. Halfway through she got stuck. Destiny grabbed her hands and pulled her through.

"Which way?" the spy asked.

Noelle pointed. She hurried to keep up with the long-legged agent. They hugged the walls of the buildings and stayed in the shadows as much as possible. Why couldn't they make a straight beeline for the carousel? With the light of the full moon and the security lamps atop the poles, they didn't need their flashlights. The guard shack was up ahead. Through the building's window came the sounds of the high school basketball game on the radio. With the guard engaged in following the boys in the red-and-green jerseys, he wouldn't hear them if they fell over a garbage can. Nevertheless, the women couched low as they passed beneath the shack window.

With the rides immobile, the neon lights off and the grounds empty of people, the park felt more like a Halloween spook house than a Christmas fun place. The rides looked like giant spiders with tentacles. Despite her jacket, Noelle shivered. A few more yards and they'd be near the merry-go-round. A quick look for the microdot and then back to the car. Noelle might be home in time to catch the second half of the ball game.

They passed by a large, windowless building. Noelle

sniffed. An unpleasant odor emanated from inside the building. "Hey, Destiny!"

"I told you to hush."

"Is Hanover's first name Dasher? Like Santa's reindeer?"

"Why are you thinking of that at a time like this?"

"We're standing by the barn where they keep the live reindeer. You remember the names of Santa's reindeer. On Dasher, on Dancer, on Prancer and Vixen—"

"Okay, his name's Dasher. If you ever call him that, I'll deny that I told you. Now will you keep your mind on the mission?"

Noelle grinned and wondered how Hanover would react if she did call him Dasher. That might make him grumpier than usual. As they moved away from the barn, Destiny grabbed her partner's hand and pulled her behind the snow-cone hut.

"What's wrong?" Noelle whispered. "We're here. The carousel is right ahead of us."

"Somebody beat us to it."

Noelle peeked around the corner of the building. A security light towered over the majestic merry-go-round and its army of giant animals and birds. A figure in a trench coat stood silhouetted against the light. Noelle couldn't see his face. The mystery man ran his hand along the rump of the carousel's black horse. He pried at one of the stones with a penknife.

Noelle draw back. "Who's that?"

"Sure ain't Santy Claus. Might be the guy who intercepted your phone call."

"So I screwed up again. I'm sorry. Everything I do is wrong."

"Shut up! Throw a pity party on your own time."

"What do we do now? Go home?"

"We don't give up. That's SIAMESE rule number

one."

"What's rule number two?"

"If someone has what you want, you take it from him."

The figure slipped the penknife and the stone into his right coat pocket and moved away.

"He's got it," said Destiny. "Now we get *him*. If he leaves the ground, we've lost the data. Our car's too far away to go after him."

The figure slinked away. In their hurry, the women didn't bother to hide but ran out in the open. The man glanced behind his shoulder at them and sped up. The women ran faster. He turned left behind a building. The women did the same and stopped.

Their prey had vanished.

Noelle's heart sank. To think she'd come this far and worked so hard to lose a simple game of tag.

Destiny broke into her thoughts. "You know this place. If you were on the lam, where would you hide?"

The alleyway was tucked between two long buildings; a wall blocked the far end of the corridor to create a dead end. "He didn't have time to climb the wall," said Noelle. "The wall's too high to jump and he'd need a ladder. If he ran up one of the fire escapes, we'd see him." She pointed to a basement door to her left. "This door is the nearest escape route, but it's always locked."

"Locks are kid's play for a spy."

The women went down the five steps leading to the basement. Sure enough, the door knob had been sawed out and left on the ground. Destiny stuck her fingers in the hole and pulled the door open. Inside, Noelle reached for a wall switch to turn on the lights, but Destiny grabbed her hand. The spy switched on her penlight and the narrow beam provided ample light. Noelle turned on her lantern and the big lens emitted a wide, unfocused ray of light.

"Keep your light low and listen for footsteps," said Destiny.

They inched through the dark kitchen, alert for any sound. They passed the long counters and metal tables where food was prepared for the diners. They aimed their lights into the various cabinets and under the tables but found no one. They moved into a hallway. On the left stood a linen closet. Destiny opened the door and they peered inside. The door behind them, across the corridor, silently opened. A figure stepped out and pushed them into the linen closet, shutting the door behind them. The women sprawled on the floor.

Destiny stood and pulled her partner to her feet. "Noelle! Are you all right?"

"Yeah, what happened?"

"He got the drop on us." She picked up her penlight, turned it off, and flipped on the room's light switch. "Rule number three: always pay attention to your surroundings."

"You let your guard down. This time *you* messed up."

Destiny glared at her.

The spy twisted the doorknob. The knob didn't budge. She squatted and inspected the keyhole. "The creep filled in the lock with epoxy."

"How do you know?"

"That's what I would have done."

Noelle glanced around the small room. No other doors or windows, just floor-to-ceiling wall shelves holding white tablecloths, linen napkins and kitchen towels. "So we're trapped."

"Thanks for that news flash." Destiny didn't sound happy.

A white vapor seeped into the room from beneath the door. Destiny got up quickly and shoved Noelle against the far wall.

   She shouted, "Poison gas!"

Chapter 24: Fun, Fun, Fun

"Don't breathe. Don't talk," Destiny said.

The toxic gas choked Noelle. The foul-smelling fumes made her dizzy. She wobbled and placed a hand on a shelf of hand towels to steady herself.

Destiny yanked off her scarf and ripped the material in two. She handed one piece to her partner. "Tie this around your face. It'll screen out the gas for a few minutes."

Noelle wrapped the cloth over her mouth and nose and knotted the scarf behind her head. By taking shallow breaths she could barely stay conscious. The white haze of gas had risen to their knees. Destiny removed her earrings. Noelle frowned. They were facing certain death, and her partner was fussing with her jewelry? The spy squashed the earrings between her palms, kneaded the putty-like substance, and pressed the sticky stuff over the keyhole.

While Destiny worked, she did a countdown. "Ten, nine, eight, seven, six . . . Stand back!"

As Noelle moved away from the door, Destiny continued. "Five, four, three, two . . ."

The putty exploded.

Destiny kicked the door open and ran into the hall. Noelle didn't need a command to follow. Several yards down the hall, the women stopped and tore off the scarves, coughing and gasping for fresh air.

Off Noelle's puzzled look, Destiny explained. "I told you everything I wear is good for something. The earrings were plastic explosives. After they're crushed,

I have ten seconds before it all goes boom."

"Remind me to never shop at your jewelers."

"You'd be a blast at parties."

"So where did the bum go?"

"Outside. If he thinks we're dead, he wouldn't want to hang around when someone finds the bodies."

Noelle watched the white vapor swirling down the hall. "The gas. It'll affect the employees when they come to work in the morning."

"No, in this long hallway it'll dissipate in an hour or two. Come on!"

They retraced their steps to the basement door where they had come in.

"I left my flashlight back here," Noelle said.

"Good riddance."

"But my name's on my flashlight. If someone finds it—"

"Then you think up a good explanation. Come on, second banana. We gotta split."

Noelle realized she couldn't return in the morning and retrieve her lost flashlight because the kitchen staff arrived hours before the park opened. Someone was bound to find it. But for now, her top worry was to get out of the park alive.

They ran a few yards until Destiny stopped. "We can't outrun him. We'll have to intercept. Think, Noelle. What's the quickest way out of here without going past the guard shack?"

Noelle caught her breath before answering. "The fastest route is straight ahead, but that leads to the main guest parking lot, and I bet he didn't park there. I think he left his car along the service road and came through the fence like we did. He's heading to the north side of the park."

"Show me."

This time Noelle took the lead. They sprinted. "I

think we have about ten, fifteen minutes before the guard makes his rounds again."

Destiny nodded, her eyes scanning ahead for the enemy.

Noelle turned to her right. "This way's a short cut to the fence."

They circled behind the Doll House, a small cottage full of miniatures and antique dolls, and ended up on a large grassy square in front of the store. The Elves Toy Workshop (where guests watched toymakers ply their craft) and The Glassworks (full of handmade glass ornaments for sale) also faced the square. On the opposite side of the lawn stood the Holiday Funhouse, a ride-through spook house without the scares. To the right of the square ran the chain-link fence that marked the park's boundary. Their assailant ran into the middle of the grassy area and stopped. The women moved between him and the fence, cutting off his escape route. He stood still. His eyes darted about, searching for an exit. Noelle finally got a glimpse of their foe—and was disappointed. He was just an ordinary guy, without the beady eyes or wicked leer or cheek scar or pockmarked face of a pulp fiction villain. The man was average height with dark hair and an undistinguished face. If she met him on the street in daylight she'd pay no attention to him. But the one feature that struck her were the eyes that sent a chill down her spine. The windows to his soul were void of expression—no fear, hesitation, anxiety or even hate. She's never seen anyone with such empty eyes.

"Give us the microdot!" Destiny shouted.

The man ran into the funhouse.

Destiny started after him, but her foot caught on the three-inch-high fencing that lined both sides of the walkway. She fell forward onto the concrete pavement.

Noelle rushed to her side. "Are you all right?"

Destiny tried to stand. "I busted my ankle." Noelle grabbed her partner's arm to lift her up, but Destiny shook her head. "I can't run. You'll have to get the microdot."

"Me!"

"You see anyone else around?"

"I'm supposed to say 'please' and he'll hand it over?"

The spy removed the handgun from her belt holster. "Use this."

Noelle's eyes grew big. She took a step back. "I can't shoot a man!"

"You gotta do it."

"But it's wrong! Murder is a sin!"

"It's homicide, self defense. Big difference from murder. Either you shoot first or he does. I'd rather you be the one who comes out alive."

"I've never used a gun before. I don't know how."

Destiny's mouth turned down. "Point. Squeeze the trigger gently. Now go. You're wasting time."

"Destiny, I can't do it."

"GO!" This time the spy didn't bother to keep her voice down.

Noelle wrapped her fingers around the cold metal of the gun. It felt heavy, clunky and evil. She stuck the weapon in her pants pocket, her mind reeling. Kill someone! Even if she retrieved the microdot, she'd land in jail for murder. But she couldn't leave her partner in the lurch. And Destiny was right about one thing. The man had to eventually leave the funhouse, and when he did he wouldn't hesitate to use his weapon on them.

Noelle took a deep breath and darted up the metal stairs leading to the funhouse entrance. The guests rode through the attraction in open cars that resembled Santa's sleigh. A track for the cars ran across the front of the building and turned inside. She stepped over the track and entered the funhouse. She wished Destiny had given her the flashlight as well—Noelle couldn't see a thing in the darkness. What if the man was hiding in the shadows, ready to pounce? She felt along the wall for the power lever that turned on the lights—and activated the ride. She pushed up the switch and the building became alive. Rows of tiny colored lights blinked along the interior walls. The track rumbled, and the cars began to move. Along one wall ran a narrow ledge where the maintenance crew stood to make repairs. As the first car nudged her legs, Noelle jumped aside and landed on the ledge. A recorded tape with an irritating instrumental version of "Here We Come A-wassailing" kicked on. The music blared from numerous speakers set in the walls. Noelle wanted to switch off the noise, but she had no time to search for the control switch or button that regulated the music.

As the cars clanked past, Noelle pressed her back against the wall and inched along the ledge. The man had only a few places to hide. Had he already left the funhouse and the park? Giant plastic snowflakes on wires dropped from the ceiling. Noelle ducked, barely missing one. She tried to recall the various gags that occurred during the ride so she could avoid them. The next, if she remembered correctly, would be a blast of freezing cold air mixed with ice pellets to simulate a snowstorm. She approached the nozzles embedded in the walls. She waited until the tubes shot their chilly contents, and stepped around the hoses before the next car arrived.

But she didn't move fast enough to evade the garland grabbers, strips of artificial greenery propelled from wall tubes. The lengthy green cords wrapped around her legs and torso. Frustrated by the delay, she struggled to rip the strips off her body. Noelle reached the emergency door that provided a quick way out for scared or queasy guests. The door lock was secure and intact, so the spy had not left this way. He must still be inside the funhouse—but where?

Panels of colored neon lights along the wall switched on. Her eyes had grown used to the darkness, and the onslaught of brightness dazed her. The neon tubes were shaped as candles, stockings, wreaths and gift-wrapped boxes. Noelle held a hand over her eyes and squinted as the neon blinked on and off—that's why she didn't see the man crouched in the oncoming car.

As the car pulled closer to Noelle, he jumped. She yelled in surprise as he grabbed her arms. A wave of fright hit, but she pushed it aside. Using the self-defense lessons she had learned at SIAMESE headquarters, she kicked at his shin and butted her forehead into his face. He pressed his body against her, pushing her against the wall. With one hand he grabbed her throat. The narrow ledge barely had room for the two. Noelle twisted to one side to escape the throat hold, and she lost her balance. As she pitched forward she grabbed the man, taking him off the ledge with her.

They didn't fall on the track. At this point of the ride, the cars tilted to drop the riders into a giant rotating barrel. The guests then slid down the walls of the slanted barrel to the ride's end. The pair landed hard onto the barrel's interior. The man cushioned the fall for Noelle, but she still felt rattled. The movement of the barrel separated them. Noelle slid downward. She had to get close to the man and retrieve the microdot. He tried to stand, but the churning floor knocked him down. Noelle knew better than to get on her feet. She crawled on her belly, but the moving floor kept her from closing in on the man. The umpteenth repetition of the tinny-sounding carol nearly made her scream. The foe scrambled away on his hands and knees. Then the barrel rolled faster and he slid toward Noelle. As she reached for his coat, he tumbled away, flipping over and over. The ride was almost over. A few more feet and they'd be scraping the bottom of the barrel. Once the man reached the loading platform, he'd run. It was now or never.

Noelle crouched and sprang toward the man. But instead of falling on him she banged her head on one of the giant plastic reindeer that hung from the ceiling and swung to and fro like a pendulum. She landed on her seat and slid out of the barrel, falling onto the cushioned mat beside the car track. The man was already standing. He pulled a gun from a shoulder holster beneath his coat. At the sight of a gun barrel pointed at her, Noelle froze. But just for a second. She ducked behind one of the three-foot high concrete posts, barriers to keep folks from entering the ride via the exit. A sharp pain ripped through her upper left arm. A spot of blood formed on her sleeve. She sat on her heels and pressed her palm on the wound to stop the bleeding. A second bullet pinged off the post in front of her. The next bullet would kill her. No time to stop and tend to her injury.

Noelle pulled the gun from her pocket. She held the weapon tight in both hands and stuck her arms straight out, pointing at the man. *Even if he gets away, I can't kill him. That's wrong. He's a human being. I'll just hurt him. I'll scare him away with a shot.* She closed her eyes, turned her head, and fired.

Chapter 25: Where Were You When I Needed You?

The force of the weapon firing jerked her hands upward. The gunshot reverberated in her ears like a cannon roar. Then came a crash, a cry of alarm and the thump of a body falling. Had she killed the man? Her heart pounded louder that the bass in the music still blasting from the speakers. Noelle's hands shook as she pocketed the gun. She peered around the post.

The bullet had sliced through the strap that held one of the mock reindeer. The plastic prop had fallen on the spy, pinning him to the floor on his back. The man squirmed and tried to push the heavy beast off him. Bits of broken plastic reindeer legs lay strew around him. Noelle got to her feet. From the corner of her eye, she caught a flashlight beam. The park guard must be making his rounds and was on his way to investigate. Noelle had to move fast, as she had no desire to spend the rest of the night answering questions in the security shack.

The spy, the gun still in his hand, raised his arm to take another shot at Noelle, but she stomped on his hand. His fingers uncurled from around the weapon. She kicked the gun away. She'd had enough of filthy firearms for one night. She leaned over and rummaged through his coat pocket. The man tried to stop her, but the broken reindeer held him down.

"Get this thing off me and we can talk." He sounded more like a wounded man than a criminal. He didn't curse or scream. Did she detect a trace of an accent? Hard to hear over the music.

"I don't trust you," she said.

"We can make a deal for the microdot. I won't kill you. I promise."

Noelle paused. He sounded like a pleasant man, not at all threatening. She grabbed the body of the broken reindeer to move it off. Then she looked into his face. His eyes showed no panic or kindness, just the coldness of a harden spy. He was lying. She remembered what Hanover had told her: *I call it healthy suspicion. The first rule I learned as an agent was that people are not always what they seem to be.*

The flashlight beam moved closer. Noelle let go of the plastic animal and instead jammed her hand into the man's pocket. She found the red stone from the carousel. For good measure, she took his wallet as well. Noelle crammed both items into her pants pocket and ran. The guard turned the corner onto the grassy lawn. She grabbed the porch railing in front of the Doll House, vaulted over, and huddled in the shadows. The guard stared at the lit up, noisy funhouse and then noticed the spy. He hoisted the broken prop off the man and knelt beside him. The guard talked to the man. Noelle strained to listen, but the funhouse music drowned out his words.

A pebble bonked Noelle on the head. She rubbed her scalp and turned. Destiny had crawled up to the railing. She motioned for Noelle to come. Noelle glanced at the guard. He had his back to her and was speaking into his walkie-talkie. With the guard distracted, Noelle climbed over the railing.

Noelle held out the handgun with a finger and thumb. "Here. Take this nasty thing."

"That nasty thing saved our lives." Destiny returned the weapon to her belt holster.

Noelle helped her partner to stand, with one arm around Destiny's waist. Together they hobbled to the opening in the fence. This time Noelle crawled through the hole first and eased Destiny through. They stood by the car.

"Looks like you got nicked." Destiny nodded at the splotch of blood on Noelle's sleeve.

"Yeah, it hurts." She held her wounded arm. "Should we look for the spy's car? It could be full of clues."

"No way. In two minutes this place will be swarming with cops, CIA and reporters. You gotta get home and set up an alibi."

"Can you drive with that bum foot?"

Destiny shrugged. "I've had worse." With one hand on the car to steady her, she limped to the driver's side door. From the highway came the wail of a police car.

Once they were inside the car, Noelle said, "Go down on this road till you reach a turn-off on the left. That's Old Stokes Road. The road circles Yuletide and eventually ends up near my house. We'll miss the cops coming in on the main drag."

Destiny started the car. "Sounds good. What about the microdot?"

Noelle grinned from ear to ear. "I got it!"

Destiny smiled as well. "I knew you would."

Saturday

After she had given Ceebee his first feeding of the day and let him outside, Noelle sat on the edge of her bed, pushed up the sleeve of her pajama top, and inspected the gauze wrapped around her upper arm. When the women had returned from the theme park, Noelle had dragged out her Girl Scout first-aid kit. Destiny cleaned the bullet hole with iodine and bandaged it. Fortunately, the bullet had only nicked her and was not lodged inside the limb, so Noelle was spared a hospital visit and a slew of sticky questions from the nurses. The weather was cool enough that she could hide the bandage with long sleeves.

Noelle threw on a bathrobe and slippers and headed for the kitchenette. She turned on the radio for the news and listened while she toasted a brown sugar cinnamon Pop-Tart and nursed a glass of orange juice. According to the WEEK-AM report, the police had arrested an unknown man for trespassing onto the theme park. He carried no identification and refused to give his name. The man was taken to the police station, where he died of a heart attack. The police concluded he was a homeless man looking for shelter at the park. End of the story.

Noelle was grateful she wasn't the one who'd killed him, but she still felt sorry for his untimely death. She was thankful he didn't spill the beans about her presence at the park, but she felt annoyed that the press was taking the incident so lightly. Homeless, indeed. He'd probably end up in a pauper's grave in a strange town far from his home and family. Did his family know where he was that night or even his occupation? Would anyone weep over his demise? If he had gone into an honest line of work and hadn't become a cold-blooded spy, who knows what kind of great things he might have done for his community.

The phone rang. The last person Noelle wanted to talk to this morning was on the other end. Trevor Spellman wanted to know what she knew about the park break-in.

"What break-in? I was home reading a book."

"On the night of a home game? C'mon, Noelle, when we were in school you never missed the Elves in action."

"I was tired. I had a busy week."

"Then who was the other person at the park last

night?"

"What are you talking about?"

"At least two people were on the grounds, and they did not arrive together."

Her heart thumped faster, but she kept her voice calm. "What makes you say that?"

"I went to the park this morning. I found where the back fence had been cut in two places. Why would one man need to cut two holes several yards apart? And how did that plastic reindeer at the funhouse just happen to fall on the guy's noggin?"

"Things wear out."

"Sure they do. The rides at the park have never malfunctioned. I checked the maintenance records at the park office. The funhouse was inspected just three weeks ago, and the worn parts were replaced right away. Besides, if a homeless man didn't want to attract attention, why would he turn on the noisiest attraction in the park?"

"Maybe he wanted to visit the funhouse but he didn't have time to stand in line when the park was busy."

"You should write jokes for Bob Hope." Trevor continued. "I also went to the police station and saw the booking photo of the guy. Clean shaven. Nice clothes. Not skinny or sickly. You can't tell me he was a homeless bum. So who was he?"

"I honestly don't know his name, and that's the truth." Noelle had not looked inside the man's wallet before she had handed it over to Destiny.

"Another point is he did not die of a heart attack. The doctor at the hospital thinks the man was poisoned."

"Poisoned?" This fact surprised her.

"The doc said the smell of cyanide is not hard to miss. He sent some blood samples to a police lab for testing."

"Who would want to poison a homeless man?"

"Maybe he did it himself. The cops said right before the man died, he asked for a glass of water so he could take some medicine. He swallowed a pill and died. I know you're thinking what I'm thinking. A suicide pill."

Noelle gasped. That made sense. Destiny had told her that if agents fell into enemy hands with no hope of escape, their orders were to kill themselves rather than divulge secrets.

"Maybe he had a bad reaction to the pill." She didn't sound convincing, not even to herself. "Or he really did have a heart attack."

"A guy that young and in fit condition?"

"What do you want me to say, Trevor? Sounds like you've figured everything out for yourself."

"I have all these loose threads, but I can't seem to tie them together. I'm fishing for information, but nobody's taking the bait. What's going on, Noelle?"

"If—I'm saying *if*—another person had been at the park, why do you suspect me?"

"Because you've been acting so weird lately. Ever since that stranger showed up at your doorstep, peculiar things have been going on. Somehow it all links back to you, but I can't connect the dots."

Knowing Trevor and his tenacity, he'd keep digging until he unearthed the truth. Wouldn't it be better to give him the straight scoop before he heard some garbled hearsay? But after last night's successful mission, she didn't want to jeopardize her relationship with SIAMESE.

"Look, Trevor, I really value our friendship. I don't want you to hate me for being so tight lipped, but I just can't help you. Please stop asking questions I can't answer."

"So you do know what's going on."

"All right, I do, but I can't say what it is."

A pause. "Can you tell me off the record?"

Even after a few hours of deep sleep, she still felt tired and irritable. "Not now, Trevor."

He turned on the sarcasm. "Thanks so much for your cooperation, Noelle. Now I know whom I can trust. Some pal you are." He slammed down the phone.

She hung up, dismayed. She hated to hurt a good friend. What could she do to get back in Trevor's good graces? So many secrets, and they were driving her crazy. Someday she was going to pop wide open and blab, regardless of Hanover's instructions. Noelle couldn't keep things bottled up for long.

In the meantime, something Trevor had said nagged at her—the stranger at her door. Noelle still hadn't solved the mystery of who murdered Kent Calvert. Now that all the microdots were safe with SIAMESE, she could concentrate on finding the killer. But where to start? She called the police station. The officer on duty said the Calvert case had "no new developments," meaning nobody was putting any effort into the investigation. Next week she had to return to her job at the record store, so she only had this weekend to solve the crime.

She drew a hot bath and poured a capful of Mr. Bubble into the tub. A soothing soak would wash off the night's grime, ease her sore muscles and help her think. She set a transistor radio on the bathroom sink, switched on the rock-and-roll station, and adjusted the long metal antenna. Noelle pulled off her clothes, snapped on a plastic shower cap, and stepped into the warm water. With an inflated plastic pillow under her head, she settled in the tub—careful not to let the bandage on her arm get wet—and let her mind roam. She reminisced about the night Kent showed up: his clothes, his actions, and the contents of his wallet. What had she missed? A guy on a journey—where was he going and why?

She sat up, sloshing water onto the floor. Of course! The clue was not what she had seen but what she had *not* seen. A needed piece was still missing.

Chapter 26: Searchin'

Noelle finished her bath and stepped out of the tub. She pulled the rubber drain stopper, dried off and quickly dressed in a long-sleeved, plaid flannel shirt, dungarees and canvas tennis shoes—she had a dirty job to do. A light rain was falling, so she put on a plastic windbreaker and pulled the hood over her head before driving to the hippie farm.

Moonbaby was on her knees in the vegetable garden behind the house, digging up weeds with a metal spade and oblivious to the precipitation. "What's happening, babe? You look strung out."

"Hi, Moonbaby. I hate to barge in on you like this, but I have a huge favor to ask."

"Lay it on me."

"Remember last Friday when the hitchhiker was at your house? You said he was carrying a duffle bag, right?"

"Yeah, he was totin' a bag with his stuff."

"You're positive he had a bag?"

"For real. Why?"

Noelle smiled and clapped her hands. "When Kent arrived at my house, he had no luggage. He didn't drop the bag in my yard. I think he left it along the road on his way to my place. The duffle might have a clue about the killer's identity. Can you join me on a hunting expedition to find it?"

The hippie pushed a lock of wet hair out of her eyes. "Shoot, it's a good mile or two from here to your pad. That's a lot of land to cover."

"Not really. With a bullet in him, Kent couldn't go far."

"But that was a long time ago." To a hippie, anything over a day was a 'long time.' "Someone might have snagged the bag by now. Or a critter chewed it up. Or the killer kept it as a souvenir."

"That's a chance we'll have to take. If the murderer had time to get rid of the bag, he would have dumped the body as well. Anyway, we still need to look."

"What do you mean, 'we'?"

"You know what the duffle looks like and I don't. Beside, three people can search faster than one, and I have to wrap this up before I go to work tonight."

"You want me to recruit Rambler as well?"

"It'd do him good to do some honest work for a change."

Moonbaby laughed. "You got that right, babe." She wearily got to her feet and wiped the mud off the knees of her baggy drawstring pants. "Rambler's at the head shop. I'll call and see if I can get him to haul his butt over here."

Moonbaby phoned Rambler. He wasn't thrilled with the idea of slogging though the weeds in the rain, but any excuse to get out of the shop suited him. Noelle drove home and parked, and the hippies soon joined her. The plan was to start at Noelle's cottage and work their way along Ornament Lane toward the hippie haven. Noelle searched the south side of the road. Rambler perused the area on the north. Moonbaby followed in the hearse so she could give them a lift back to the cottage. Noelle pushed back the tall grass and peered behind the trees. At least the duffle wouldn't be buried under mounds of snow or autumn leaves. Still, finding the bag a week after the fact was a long shot, and the constant drizzle made her wet and irritable.

Along the way Noelle saw crumpled paper bags, empty soft drink cups, theme park ticket stubs and chewing gum wrappers. She kicked the trash out of her path. What a messy bunch of motorists. She kept checking her watch as the sun sank in the sky. Soon she'd have to quit and go to work with or without the bag. Perhaps the luggage was long gone and they were wasting their time.

"Hey!" Rambler waved both arms. "I think I got something!"

Noelle motioned for Moonbaby to stop. She waited for another car to zip by and then ran across the street to join Rambler. Rainwater dripped from his hair and beard. Did these hippies ever dress for the weather? He pointed to a battered brown duffle bag wedged against a tree trunk.

Noelle knelt on the wet grass and pulled back her jacket hood to get a closer look. Attached to the bag handle was a luggage tag with Kent's name and Riverbend address. "This is it! Good job of spotting it, Rambler."

"I didn't see it exactly. I tripped over it."

Noelle lifted the hefty duffle, surprised by its weight. How did Kent manage to carry the heavy bag in the storm? The rainwater was leaving spots on the canvas. But something else had caused the dark brown splotches on the material.

"This looks like dried blood," said Noelle. "Maybe this was the place where he was shot."

"Man, this is too freaky for me," said Rambler. "Me and my woman are gonna burn rubber out of here."

"Sure, we're done," said Noelle. "Thanks for your help."

Noelle carried the duffle to the hearse, and Moonbaby dropped off the amateur sleuth at her house. Inside the cottage, Noelle pulled off her wet jacket, sat on the living room floor, and dumped out the duffle's contents. If she hurried, she'd have time for a quick peek inside the bag before leaving for the theme park. The duffle had clothes, a shaving kit, socks, a folded map but nothing special. A red marker had traced a certain route on the map leading to Kent's planned destination. She pawed around until she found one particular item that shouldn't have been in the bag at all.

Could this be the clue that identified Kent's killer?

She called the police station and, to her surprise, found Chief Whitlock at his desk. He was rarely around his office on Friday afternoons. She told him about her find, but he was less than enthusiastic. Since a civilian had searched the bag and not an officer with a warrant, he said, it's likely the luggage would be thrown out of court as evidence. Also, the item that Noelle found didn't prove who killed the boy. The chief said Kent could have picked up the item anywhere in town. Noelle argued that wasn't true, but Whitlock remained unconvinced.

"Can you interview the suspect?" she asked.

"I could, but it wouldn't do any good. I'd never get a confession. That's what I'd need before I could make an arrest."

After Noelle hung up, she pondered those words. Then she made another call.

Hanover listened with more interest than she expected. "That's good sleuthing, Miss McNabb. Your deduction is sound, but the police chief is right. What you have is circumstantial evidence that, by itself, won't hold up in court."

"I was hoping you could help me. You guys are good at making people give you information."

"Now hold on. We do not interrogate people based on hunches."

"I don't mean beating them with rubber hoses. I mean setting a trap for the killer. Make the murderer confess without him realizing what's going on. You know, like on *Mission: Impossible* when the good guys fool the baddie with one of their scams."

"Let me think on this, Noelle. I'll get back with you."

Noelle hung up with barely enough time to drive to the theme park. She couldn't spare the minutes to change out of her dirty clothes but that didn't matter, since the public would only see her in a clean costume. The park seemed much different today than from the night before. The loud noises, bright lights and crowds seemed unreal. No evidence of the spy chase save for a sign in front of the funhouse that read, "Closed for maintenance." A crowd of tourists stood in front of the dark and silent building, taking pictures of the notorious crime scene. Noelle didn't check to see if the holes in the fence had been repaired—someone might wonder why she was snooping around the park border.

When she reached the dressing room, the stage manager handed her a brown paper bag. "One of the janitors found this when he was cleaning this morning."

Noelle peeked inside the bag. Her flashlight! She was happy to get it back, but the manager squinted one eye and stared at her.

She pretended to be surprised. "There it is! I wondered what happened to it. One of the cooks borrowed it for a camping trip months ago. I'd forgotten all about it."

He didn't sound convinced. "If you say so. Hurry up and get dressed. You're on in fifteen minutes."

She nodded and rushed into the dressing room. Let him think what he might. The flashlight didn't prove she was on the grounds last night. Noelle put on her makeup and costume and performed for full houses.

News of the "homeless man" had pulled in the tourists. Between the shows, the cast and crew gossiped about the break-in. Noelle nearly bit off her tongue to keep from telling what she knew. She finally wandered off to a quiet corner backstage to avoid the others.

When she arrived home from work, Hanover called to describe the scheme he'd concocted to flush out Kent Calvert's killer.

"That's brilliant!" she said. "It's so crazy it just might work!"

Chapter 27: All Together Now
Sunday

Before and after Sunday School, the actress was busy. As per Hanover's instructions, Noelle invited as many people as she could to a special party she was throwing that evening "just for fun."

"It's been so gloomy with the rain and no holidays to celebrate," she explained, "so I thought we'd get together at The Barn for a indoor barbecue to brighten up the day."

Nobody in Yuletide ever said no to free food, so everyone accepted the invitation.

Just before the worship service, Noelle sat with her family in the sanctuary pew and told her mother about the party.

"This is a surprise." Mom was so perceptive. "You've never hosted a big wingding before."

"Maybe it's time I did."

"But on such short notice? People like to make plans in advance."

"Mom, it's Sunday night. The only thing that ever happens in this town on a Sunday night is watching Ed Sullivan on TV."

"How are you paying for it? You told me you were just scraping by."

How would she explain that SIAMESE was footing the bill? "One of the guests at the park really liked the show and gave me a big tip."

Noelle grabbed a hymnal from the rack in the back of the pew in front of her and flipped the pages to the first hymn. She buried her face in the book so her mother wouldn't see her reddening cheeks. She'd told a lie in church! If she were Catholic, she'd be marching straight for the confessional. Mom started to say something, but the opening notes of the organ prelude drowned her out.

After the service, Noelle rushed home to call up certain people who hadn't shown up at church. All of them accepted her invitation. Then Noelle changed into a suitable party outfit: a red miniskirt with lace trim and a ribbon sash, along with white gloves and a small matching hat with cloth flowers. Not what one normally wore to a barbecue, but if the scheme worked, she'd look grand as she unmasked Kent Calvert's killer. Ceebee jumped on the bed and fussed at her. Noelle took a moment to scratch his neck and throat. He tilted his head back, regaling in the petting.

"What's the matter, sweetie? Mommy's been so busy she's been neglecting you. As soon as this is over, I'll spend more time with you. I'll teach you a new trick."

She headed for the door. Ceebee followed. Once outside, the cat didn't head into the woods but stayed on her heels. She'd parked outside the garage since she was heading back into town. The cat stood by the car door and meowed.

"What? You stay here and catch a mouse."

Noelle opened the door, and the pet jumped into the car.

"Ceebee! Get out! You can't go with me."

The cat crawled under the front seat.

"I don't have time to fish you out! Now come on!"

Ceebee yowled to let her know he wasn't moving.

"Fine. Be that way. If you want to sit in the car all day, that's your funeral."

Noelle drove off. Maybe Ceebee thought they were

headed on one of their trips to a nearby pond. A farmer owned the land, but he didn't mind the neighbors enjoying the water as long as they didn't leave litter or caused a wildfire. In the hot, humid summer, Noelle preferred swimming in the quiet, algae-laden pond rather that the city pool crammed with screaming kids. But if that's where Ceebee thought they were going, he was sadly mistaken.

The rain stopped and the clouds cleared away to permit a flood of sunshine, just the right weather for a party. Noelle arrived at The Barn before the guests showed up. As she opened the car door, Ceebee slipped out and ran off. "Hey! You better come back when I'm ready to leave! I'm not spending the night looking for you!" Cats could be so exasperating.

Inside the building, preparations were underway. A team of SIAMESE agents hung streamers from the ceiling and colorful banners on the wooden walls. They set up rows of rectangular dining tables and chairs as well as stands with floral arrangements. Along one wall ran a long buffet table with paper plates and cups and plastic silverware as well as steamer trays and empty platters for the food. Behind the serving window in the wall, other agents were preparing a feast in the kitchen. The aroma of slow-cooked barbecue chicken and beef filled the room.

In one corner, Noelle found Hanover holding a clipboard and wearing a microphone headset. "You've got quite an operation going on here," she said.

"This is nothing," he replied. "Most of our assignments are far more complex."

"You set this up overnight?"

"Most of our work is done under pressure."

They sat at a table. Hanover explained how the plan would unfold and Noelle's role in it.

When he finished, she said, "This sounds like a

gas!"

"Don't get cocky. The target might fight back when exposed. A person who's killed once has already crossed moral boundaries and will not hesitate to do it again."

"Do you mean my family and friends might be in danger?"

"That's possible. Do you want to abort the mission? We can cancel before the guests arrive."

"You'll be here to protect us, won't you?"

"No. I have other responsibilities at headquarters. Besides, I can't risk exposing myself. No one must know that SIAMESE is behind this event." Off her look he added, "Don't worry. Agent King will be here."

"I don't see her."

"She'll arrive at the appropriate time. Besides, you have plenty of street smarts yourself. You'll be fine."

She smiled at his words of confidence. Before she could say more, Hanover began talking into his headset. He rose and crossed the room to oversee the other agents. Noelle went over the plan in her head to make sure she knew it well. If she messed up, her guests might be harmed. Had she unwittingly lured the townsfolk into a death trap?

With the preparations completed, Hanover and most of his crew left, leaving only a handful of chefs in the kitchen to serve the food and a DJ to play Herb Alpert and the Tijuana Brass records over the loudspeakers. The disc jockey had a turntable and audio equipment set up on a table in the corner. The soft pop music started as the guests trickled in. Noelle picked up a ladle and filled glasses from a bowl of lemonade. An ice ring with cherries and lemon-and-lime slices floated in the bowl. Serving drinks gave Noelle something to do as the guests mingled. She was pleased to see that the murderer possibilities had all shown up. She'd also invited a number of friends and acquaintances to flesh out the party so the suspects didn't look so—well, suspect. Noelle wondered if she should lock the doors once everyone had arrived to keep the killer from escaping. But so far the residents were chatting and sipping lemonade and enjoying themselves as if they had no thought that a murderer might be among them.

After everyone had arrived and the aroma of the hot food was too irresistible, Noelle stepped up on the bandstand. She didn't have a microphone, but with her actor's training her strong, deep voice carried throughout the room.

"Excuse me, can I have everyone's attention please?" The voices subsided. "Thank you. I'd like to welcome everyone and thank you for coming today, especially on such short notice. We'll have dinner right away. And if all of you could please stick around after eating, we have some special entertainment that I think you'll enjoy." She glanced at the overstocked buffet table. "I see the food's ready to go. There's plenty, so help yourselves to seconds and thirds. Dig in!"

Noelle waited until the others had passed through the line before she filled a plate. In spite of the abundance of delicious food, she was too nervous to eat. What if her plan failed? What if she had accused the wrong person or the murderer wasn't here? What would Hanover say about wasting the money and effort for nothing? What if the 'entertainment' flopped? Would she be the laughingstock of the town? But like a good actor, she buried her feelings and kept a smile on her face. She wandered between the tables to see that everyone was happy.

Bennie bit into a drumstick. "Hey, Noelle, this is really yummy."

"Glad you like it, Bennie." She whispered in his ear. "Close your mouth when you chew."

"Yeah. Right."

May Wells and another woman were seated across the table from the soda jerk. "Noelle, have you met Vickie? She's the friend I told you about. We pledged Alpha Beta Beta the same year."

"No, I haven't." Something about the girl startled Noelle, but she didn't let on. She had seen that face before. "Nice to meet you, Vickie. Glad you could make our little shindig."

"She's down from Indy for a week or so," said May. "She drove into town last week, you know, the night of that nasty storm."

Vickie returned a hello and asked the hostess about some ruffians seated by themselves at the end of a long table. The other guests, who had dressed up for the occasion in suits and dresses, had given Vince and the bad boys a wide berth. The guys showed up in their usual tee-shirts, jeans and leather jackets.

"Excuse me, I'll go talk to them." Noelle approached the table just as Vince was taking a cigarette and lighter out of the pocket of his denim vest. "Hello, boys."

"Hey, Beanpole, how's the air up there?" Vince said.

"It's gonna get pretty smoky if you light up that cigarette."

"Oh, this thing? I gotta have it. The doctor prescribed it for my nerves." The bad boys laughed along with Vince.

"Put it away or I'll cram it up your nose."

"Ah, you wouldn't do that, skinny."

She did.

Vince coughed and sputtered as he pulled the shreds of tobacco out of his nostril. The other bad boys roared in laughter until he glared at them and they shut up.

He glowered at Noelle. "Whyja do that for?"

She smiled sweetly. "Smoking's bad for your health. Now everyone behave or I'll throw all of you outside on your rumps. Okay?" The guys gave some reluctant nods. "Fine. Enjoy your dinner, boys."

The gang didn't know that Noelle had wanted them at the party. A direct invitation would have been ignored, so she had used subterfuge. She'd invited Vince's nerdy kid brother and given him explicit instructions not to inform his sibling. Naturally, the brother had informed the bully. The bad boys thought they'd crash the party, but the joke was on them.

Noelle detoured into the kitchen to greet Moonbaby and Rambler. The hippies were uncomfortable socializing with the squares, so Noelle had set up a table in the kitchen where the hippies could eat in private without any snubbing from the hoi polloi. Back in the main room, Noelle spotted Gus E. Monty making a sales pitch to the folks at his table. On Noelle's request, someone pointed out Ted Markle, the former Yuletide resident. Noelle returned to her seat, but she'd barely started on the coleslaw when Trevor Spellman slid into the seat beside her. He wore a gray pants and a gray sports coat over a collarless red shirt.

"Something about this party smells fishy," he said.

"There's no fish, just chicken and beef."

"I don't mean the food." He tapped the side of his nose. "I've got a nose for news, and it's tingling as if I had spidey sense. You're not throwing this party for the fun of it, are you?" He said this more as a statement than a question.

"Trevor, will you relax. Not everything in life is a breaking scoop." She patted his cheek. "Settle down and eat your dinner, but keep your notebook handy when the entertainment starts."

"What have you cooked up besides the short ribs?"

"Ask me no questions, and I'll tell you no lies."

With that she turned to chat with the others at the table. The last thing she needed was Spellman interfering with her plan. She kept an eye on the guests. Many had finished eating, and the kitchen crew had started clearing away the dirty dishes. Some attendees got to their feet to stretch and head for the exit doors. Noelle had better get the show on the road before people started leaving. Leaving her half-eaten plate of food, she scrambled onto the bandstand.

"Can I have your attention, please? Thanks. Did everyone enjoy the food?" A smattering of applause. "Great. Now I'd like everyone to remain seated for a brief program. This won't take long, and it'll only work if everyone stays. I promise you'll find it amusing. Okay?"

Despite some murmurings, those standing returned to their seats. Noelle took a deep breath. So far, so good, but how long could she keep them? She nodded to the kitchen crew and they left the dining room, leaving some of the dirty dishes on the tables. Two agents set a small table in the center of the stage. They draped a red velvet cloth over the top and placed several chairs behind the table. After they left the bandstand, Noelle addressed the audience.

"And now, for your entertainment, I'm proud to present the one and only Madame Mysterioso!"

Chapter 28: Black Magic Woman

The house lights dimmed and a spotlight shone on the stage. Noelle stepped into the wings as eerie Eastern music with sitar, tabla and flute played over the loudspeakers. Fog rolled across the stage. A loud clash of cymbals, a flash of light and Madam Mysterioso—Destiny in disguise—appeared onstage, her arms folded over her chest. Noelle barely recognized her partner. The spy had silver glitter glued on her eyelids and silver stars painted on her cheeks. She wore a floor-length caftan of richly colored silk with a gold sash tied around the waist. Crystal earrings hung from her ears. Gold chains dangled from her wrists and encircled her neck. A silk scarf was tied around a wig of black dreadnoughts. Her fingers sported long red fake nails. The makeup and costume department of SIAMESE must be incredibly well stocked.

Destiny raised her arms and the long sleeves fell to her elbows. "I am Madam Mysterioso." She spoke in a deep, somber voice. "I see all. I know all. I reveal all mysteries. Tonight we will contact the sprits and ask their help to solve a puzzle that has perplexed this community. But beware—the solution to this enigma may not please you."

The guests murmured in surprise. The music faded out. The house lights came on. "I cannot contact the spirits alone. I need helpers to assist me. Do not be afraid. You will not be harmed. But you may be shocked. May I have volunteers?"

Destiny paced the front of the stage. Several people

raised their hands, but she deliberately selected certain people: Vickie, Ted Markle, Gus E. Monty, Vince and Bennie. With a little coaxing, they came on stage. Destiny seated them behind the table and facing the audience.

"Hey, what kind of lame-o game is this?" said Vince.

"Silence!" Madam snapped. "I require complete and utter quiet. The spirits may harm those who interfere with my concentration. And now . . . "

She clapped her hands twice and an agent brought in a game board along with a plastic, triangle-shaped device with a hole near the tip. The agent left. The house lights darkened again. Destiny sat behind the middle of the table with the others on her right and left. A spotlight rested on her. Noelle stood near one of the backstage exits, out of sight from the guests but where she had a clear view of the room. The bad boys were whispering among themselves. What if they started a commotion? Something furry pressed against her ankle and she looked down.

"Ceebee!" she whispered. "How did you get in here?"

The cat stared at the buffet table and sniffed. The leftovers had not been packed away, and Ceebee had caught a whiff of the meat. Noelle scooped up the cat in her arms.

Madam Mysterioso spoke. "I have with me a Ouija board, a tool to spell out the messages the spirits wish to send. We are safe. The board only summons friendly spirits, not demons. Now, all of you seated at the table, place your fingertips on the planchette. It will not bite you."

Those at the table exchanged glances, but they stretched out their hands and gingerly touched the plastic planchette.

"Rest your fingers lightly," she continued. "Do not press down or force the planchette to move. I ask all in the room to concentrate. Clear your minds and focus your thoughts on the board. The more thought energy we generate together, the clearer the message. Let us begin."

Destiny placed her own fingers on the planchette. The spooky music played softly. Madam Mysterioso closed her eyes, learned her head back and hummed. The planchette began to move across the board.

"Yes, yes! I feel the energy flowing. Good, good, everyone, keep your thoughts directed at the board. Oh spirits, we have a question for you. We cannot rest until we have an answer."

Vince grinned as he tried to push the planchette to spell a rude word. But the device bolted and the tip quickly pointed to a series of letters.

Destiny spelled out the letters aloud. "M-U-R-D-E-R."

The people in the audience talked among themselves.

"Quiet! I need complete silence! A murder has taken place in our community. Tell us, great Ouija board, what is the name of this unfortunate victim?" She spelled the letters indicated by the planchette. "K-E-N-T-C-A-L-V-E-R-T."

"This is silly," said Gus. "A board can't tell you about a murder. It's just a game."

"Who's Kent Calvert?" Bennie asked.

Destiny glared at them and resumed her singsong voice. "Mr. Calvert. Can you tell us who dispatched you to the spirit world before your appointed time to die?"

Smoke arose from behind Madam Mysterioso. Above her head an image of light appeared: the face of Kent Calvert. The guests whispered among themselves.

From the room speakers came the distorted voice of a young man.

"I died for my country but I was killed in a woods, not on a battlefield. I died for peace. I died for my beliefs and convictions. I did not die for an unjust war. I died a martyr."

From the audience someone shouted, "Liar! You lived and died as a coward!"

A second spotlight picked up the Colonel, in full dress uniform and medals, as he sprang from his chair. His eyes blazed at the dead man's image. "You were too scared to go to Vietnam and fight like a man for this glorious country! You'd rather let the commies overrun our great land with their atheistic socialism that to get your toes wet in a rice field. Sissies like you make me vomit! We don't need pantywaists like you running like rats to Canada! If I could, I'd rid this land of every last draft dodger. May you rot in hell!"

The houselights snapped on and the spotlights faded. Kent's image disappeared. Those on the stage jerked their hands off the planchette and scooted their chairs back, as if the devil himself had jumped out of the Ouija board. Every eye turned on the Army man. He blinked under the bright lights and stared at the crowd.

Destiny spoke in her normal voice, as if gently chastising a child. "Colonel, what do you know about the murder of Kent Calvert?"

A hardened look replaced the shock on Sieberson's face. He straightened his back and threw back his shoulders. "Kent Calvert? Never heard of the boy."

"Then how did you know he was a draft dodger?"

"Anyone could tell that from the way he spoke."

"You just said you want to kill all draft dodgers."

"I was speaking metaphorically."

Noelle set Ceebee on the floor and stepped out of the shadows in view of the guests. She pulled a tri-fold color glossy pamphlet from her purse and held it up for all to see. "Yesterday I found Kent Calvert's duffle on the side of Ornament Lane. He dropped the bag after he was shot. The bag has bloodstains on it, and this paper was inside. It's your pamphlet, Colonel, a paper you wrote in support of the Vietnam War. At the library you gave me some of these brochures. Remember? But you're the only person who has this pamphlet. How did this leaflet get into Kent's bag unless you gave it to him right before he died?"

A look of desperation crossed the soldier's face. Chief Whitlock pushed back his chair and began to stand up. Then the Colonel moved quickly. With one hand, he snatched a meat carving knife off the buffet table behind him. With his other hand, he pulled Mrs. McNabb to her feet. He stood behind her and clutched the woman against his chest. He placed the edge of the knife against her throat.

"Nobody move!" he said.

Chapter 29: Trip, Stumble and Fall

"Mom!" Noelle screamed.

Mr. McNabb jumped to his feet "Let her go, you fiend! Don't hurt my wife!"

"Everyone stay seated and nobody will be hurt!" Sieberson inched backward toward the exit door, keeping Mrs. McNabb between him and the crowd.

Noelle burned with rage. How dare the murderer use her mom as a hostage! But what could she do? She glanced at Destiny, who gave her a look that said, "My hands are tied." If Destiny fired her gun, she'd hit the hostage. But Noelle couldn't let the Colonel leave the building. As a trained Army man, he knew how to hide and never be seen again.

The aromas of the buffet table were too tempting for Ceebee. Nothing ever stood between the cat and food. He jumped off the stage.

"Ceebee!" Noelle called. "Come back!"

The feline made a beeline for the buffet table—and Sieberson just happened to be in the way. Ceebee ran between the man's feet and tripped him. The Colonel dropped the knife and went sprawling backward, with the hostage landing atop him. Mr. McNabb pulled his wife to safety. Ceebee jumped on the soldier's shirt and kneaded Sieberson's chest with his claws.

"Owww!" The Colonel swatted the cat. "Get this rabid creature off me!"

Ceebee laid back his ears and yowled in the man's face.

Noelle ran to fetch the cat, but the sneaky pet slid

beneath the serving table.

Whitlock helped the disgraced soldier to his feet and handed Sieberson his cane. "Colonel, I think you and me better go down to the station and have us a little talk."

The Army man turned rigid and his eyes focused off in the distance. "I will only give my name, rank and serial number."

The chief put his arm around Sieberson's shoulder and led him outside to the patrol car. After a moment of silence, chairs scraped across the tile floor as people got out of their chairs and began chattering.

Bennie jumped off the stage and ran to Noelle. "What happened? Why did the Colonel act like that?"

"Last Saturday night he shot and killed Kent Calvert."

"Who he?"

"Don't worry about it, Bennie. Just go back to the soda shop and keep making those delicious milkshakes."

He nodded and returned to his dad as Edna Apple stepped up. "That was brave of you, Noelle, taking a big chance like that. But I can't believe the Colonel would hurt anyone. He contributed every year to the veterans' fund. He always seemed like such a gentleman."

"We all have our breaking points, and I guess Kent did it for the old soldier," said Noelle.

Chris Kloss, however, was not as grateful. "That wasn't very sporting of you, Noelle, besmirching that fine man's reputation."

"Nobody is above the law, mayor," said Noelle. "Harold ruined his own name. All I did was show everyone what kind of man he really was."

"But was it right of you to do so? That good man is going to spend the rest of his life in prison with all those hardened criminals."

"Maybe the Colonel will finally realize he's no longer in the trenches, fighting the war. I don't think he was ever happy living in peacetime."

Chris tucked his thumbs under his suspenders. "I hope we can keep this out of the big city papers. We can't let folks think that Yuletide is full of mean people."

"Mayor, lighten up," she said. "One killer in a town of ten-thousand people does not make us the murder capital of the world. It shows that we're honest. If someone in our midst does something bad, we hold him accountable."

"We have a lot of fine folk here in Yuletide. Sure is a shame to have a bad apple in the bunch. I had lunch with the Colonel just the other day, and he picked up the tab." The mayor shook his head as he walked away.

May Wells gave Noelle a hug. "I'm glad you solved the crime. I've been going crazy, thinking about that poor boy who was shot."

"This may surprise you," Noelle said, "but Kent had a photo of Vickie in his wallet."

"Really?"

"I recognized her as soon as I saw her today. Maybe Kent loved her all along but the baby scared him off."

"Funny you should say that. Vickie told me she was sad about his death. She really loved him, but back then she was young and scared and her parents wanted her to finish college before she started a family. Who knows, maybe if she and Kent had gotten married and raised the baby together, he'd still be alive."

Noelle smiled. "You never know." As May and Vickie left the building, the bad boys started to follow them out.

"Hey, Vince!" Noelle called.

He turned. "Yeah, what?"

"How did you like the show?"

He gave her a thumbs-down gesture. Vince would never admit that anything Noelle did could impress him.

"Just out of curiosity, where did you get that money I saw in your hand last week?"

"Oh, that? My grandparents gave me a wad of dough for my birthday. I told them I was too old for toys and clothes and kid stuff, so just give me cash to spend." With that, the bad boys left so they could smoke outside.

Noelle turned her attention elsewhere. "Mom, are you all right?"

Her mother nodded. "Just a little shaken. I would have never guessed the Colonel would go and do something like that."

"He killed many people when he was in the Army," said Noelle. "He'd developed the ability to hurt a human being without remorse. He viewed anyone who didn't support the Vietnam War as the enemy."

"How sad," said Mom. "For the Colonel, I mean. He's a very sick man. I hope he gets treatment for his problem."

"I hope he gets a hundred years in jail!" Dad said. "Using an innocent woman as a shield and killing a young boy. That's just wrong. Noelle, is that why you set up this party? To expose the Colonel?"

The daughter nodded. "I had some circumstantial evidence, but I needed something more definite. I had to trick Harold into making a confession. With all these people as witnesses, that's pretty conclusive."

"How did you know the boy was a draft dodger?" Mom asked.

"When I found the pamphlet in Kent's bag, I finally remembered where I'd seen him before. He was on TV at the protest rally in Riverbend. I couldn't place him at first because he was standing in the back of the crowd and all I saw was his profile. But he was one of the kids burning his draft card. In his duffle bag he also had a map marked with a route to Canada. He was hitchhiking north to escape the draft. After he left the hippie pad Saturday night, the Colonel must have driven by and picked him up. I think he wanted to take Kent to the Army recruitment center and the boy didn't want to go. Everyone knows the Colonel carried a handgun in his car. I don't know if Kent asked Harold to stop the car and let him out, or if the Colonel ordered him out of the car so he wouldn't get blood on the car seat." She turned to Spellman, who was standing beside her and furiously taking dictation with pen and steno pad. "Are you getting all of this?"

Trevor kept his eyes on his pad. "Keep talking, keep talking."

The twins ran up, cute as bugs in matching playsuits. "Hey, sis, you should of blasted that guy with a phaser!" said Donny.

Dolly rolled her eyes. "Phasers aren't real. That's just a TV show."

"It's not a stupid show like your dumb Monkees. You can set a phaser to stun or kill." He pointed his finger at his twin as if holding a gun. "Zap! I stunned you!"

She slapped his hand. "Stop that!"

"I think it's time we got the twins home and in bed," said Mom. "Noelle, is there anything we can do to help you clean up here?"

"No, I'm fine." As the guests trickled out of the building, the agents had rapidly gathered up the dirty dishes, stripped the tablecloths and folded the chairs.

The McNabbs said goodbye, and soon everyone had left except for Trevor and Noelle.

"Okay, Noelle, fess up. Who the devil was that

Madam Mysterioso? Whoever she is, she's good. Is she a real conjurer or just an actress like you?"

"Here, I'll introduce you. Destiny, can you—" She glanced at the stage. Empty. "Excuse me." Noelle checked the kitchen, restrooms and backstage area. Destiny had disappeared just as quietly as she had arrived. Noelle rejoined the reporter. "I guess she left."

"Another one of your secrets. Who put on the magic show? You can't tell me you conjured up this smoke and mirrors act all by yourself."

"I know how to make stage effects for the theater."

"Right. How about that floating head?"

"Easy. Slide projector. We made a slide using Kent's photo from his driver's license."

"*We*? Who is this *we*?"

Noelle realized her slip. "Okay, so I had help."

"How did you record a dead man's voice?"

"We had to wing it with an actor. Harold had only met Kent once, and we hoped he didn't remember how the boy talked. The voice was distorted enough to fool the Colonel."

"How did you know the Ouija board would spell out the right words?"

Noelle reached into her purse and pulled out a small metal box. "Remote control. The bottom of the planchette had a set of wheels pre-programmed to move in a specific direction. I switched this on and presto!"

Trevor pocketed his steno book. "That's quite a yarn, Noelle, and you're quite a gal. Now all you have to do is tell me who concocted this nutty scheme and I can file the story."

"Sorry, but I have to run. I gotta get home and feed the cat."

"I don't think that'll be necessary." He smiled and nodded at the buffet table where Ceebee was chomping heartily on a tray of barbecued chicken breasts.

"Ceebee!" The cat raised his head and barbecue sauce dripped off his mouth. Noelle sighed. "Well, go ahead and eat. For helping me catch a killer, I suppose you deserve a treat."

Back home in the cottage, Noelle slipped out of the dress and into her pajamas, too wound up to sleep. She switched on the stereo and put on side one of the *Pet Sounds* record. Noelle collapsed on the sofa and let the gentle vibes of the Beach Boys calm her. Ceebee sat at her feet and washed up from his meaty feast. So that was that. Microfilm recovered and a murder vindicated. Maybe now her life would get back to normal. After all this excitement, playing a witch at a Christmas theme park didn't seem so bad. Maybe she should take a teaching job in the rural Indiana countryside. Directing Rogers and Hammerstein musicals with a bunch of hick town teenagers seemed rewarding enough to suit her.

The phone rang. No doubt Spellman wanted more information for his exclusive or Mom was checking up on her. Wearily she picked up the receiver.

"Hello?"

"Fido Brown calling Tabby Gray. You're needed."

THE END

ABOUT THE AUTHOR

 Sally Carpenter is a native Hoosier now living in Moorpark, California. The next Psychedelic Spy book is *Hippie Haven Homicide*.

Her other books with Cozy Cat Press are in the Sandy Fairfax Teen Idol Series: *The Baffled Beatlemaniac Caper, The Sinister Sitcom Caper*, *The Cunning Cruise Ship Caper, The Quirky Quiz Show Caper, The Notorious Noel Caper,* and *The Highland Havoc Caper. Beatlemaniac* was a 2012 Eureka! Award finalist for best first mystery novel.

Sally wrote a Sandy Fairfax short story, "The Puzzling Puppet Show Caper," for the CCP anthology, *Cozy Cat Shorts*, and chapter three for the CCP group mystery, *Chasing the Codex*. She has stories in two other anthologies: "Dark Nights at the Deluxe Drive-in," for *Last Exit to Murder* and "Faster Than a Speeding Bullet," in *Plan B: Omnibus*.

Sally has a Master of Arts Degree in theater from Indiana State University. While in school, her plays "Star Collector" and "Common Ground" were finalists in the American College Theater Festival One-Act Playwriting Competition. "Common Ground" also won a college creative writing award. "Star Collector" was produced in New York City and served as the inspiration for the Sandy Fairfax series.

Sally also has a Master of Divinity and a black belt in tae kwon do. She's worked as an actress, college writing instructor, jail chaplain and tour guide/page for Paramount Pictures in Hollywood. She's now employed at a community newspaper where she writes the Roots of Faith inspirational column.

Sally is a member of American Christian Fiction Writers and is on Facebook. To download two free short stories, go to her website: http://sandyfairfaxauthor.com.